Ariair Online: A Piece of Legend

By Craig Dunn

ARIAIR
KINGDOM OF LEIGHEST
Be
Oxgate
KINGDOM OF LYCAON
Drusaga
Djanzai
Drella
N
W
E
S

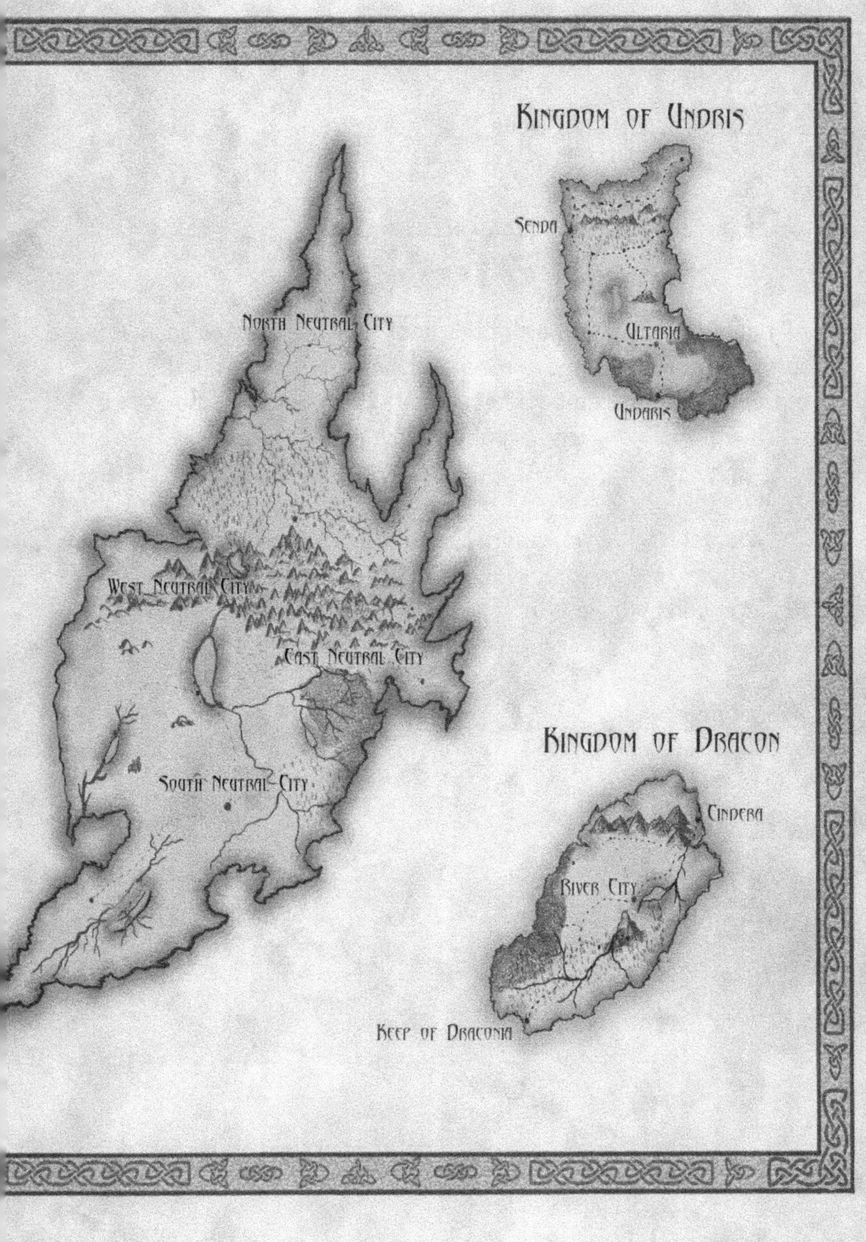

Kingdom of Undris
Senda
Ultaria
Undaris
North Neutral City
West Neutral City
East Neutral City
South Neutral City
Kingdom of Dracon
Cindera
River City
Keep of Draconia

To those who helped me create my world and write this story.

It took me long enough, right?

I value you all for the help you have given me and will hopefully give me in the future.

A big personal thanks to Jonathan for everything you did to make this a reality and I'm sorry how many times I changed my mind.

Table of Contents

Prologue: A History Lesson

"Is this really the last one?" a woman in moss green armour said, addressing a man in blue robes.

The man in blue looked out to the horizon, a grim expression on his face. "Yes. This is it. This will finish what we have worked so hard for."

He moved to step towards the edge of the cliff, overlooking the formerly stunning valley – now overrun with undead monsters. On the other side of the valley, the ruins of a desolate city valiantly tried to defy the wear of age and elements. Its former crowning glory, a temple to a long-forgotten god, stood broken.

The man's companions stepped up to the precipice beside him – a broad assortment of strange characters. Although differing vastly in race, every one of them wore a matching look of grim determination upon their faces. As the group stepped toward the edge of the cliff, large translucent bubbles surrounded them. They hopped from the ledge and felt their stomachs drop at the strange sensation of being lowered gently to the valley floor.

The bubble dissipated as soon as they found their footing on solid ground and without a word the group began to stride toward the city, taking care to avoid as many of the surrounding monsters as possible. Anxiously, several looked back toward the cliff edge.

Their heads whipped around at the sound of gravelly snarls, and a dense clattering of bones. A squad of Skeleton Soldiers, led by an armour-clad Skeleton Knight, began to rush them with wooden shields aloft and swords poised.

The companions made short work of them; their skill refined from long hours of practice fighting across the world. The man in blue withdrew his staff from the chest of the last Skeleton Soldier, as if he sensed something was wrong, he glanced back to the cliff for the first time.

The ground beneath their feet began to rumble ominously as if an incoming horde of creatures were stampeding into the clearing. As it did, a group of five warriors appeared at the spot from where the group had jumped.

The man in blue whipped his head back forwards urgently. "Get to the temple, now. We can't let them catch us before we retrieve the final orb. Mages, repel the undead – we don't have time to kill them all." Under his breath, he added, "I have to find it. I have to save her."

Clearing the valley, the group moved swiftly through the city, avoiding enemies as best they could. Without engaging in serious combat, they killed only those who obstructed their journey forward. As they neared the entrance to the temple at the centre of the city, the group could hear the sounds of battle still raging outside the city walls. The metallic clashing of swords, massive impacts of shields, and the continuous howling of different beasts echoed in their ears; their followers were getting closer.

They all stopped as they finally arrived at the temple, pausing to stare up in awe at the majestic, black marble exterior of the building. It was huge – almost entirely blocking out the light of the sun from where they stood. The building had a slanted roof, high columns, and an assortment of statues with cracked bodies and chipped faces.

Towering above all of them, the unnamed stone goddesses grandly flanked the beautiful, arching doors, wearing long, flowing togas, and intricate hairstyles.

A dozen scouts advanced through the doors, closely followed by the rest of the group. The beautiful entrance hall was still filled with the remains of broken pottery and statues; a fountain, covered in still-powered runes, trickled idly, undisturbed. The thing that drew their eye, however, was the gaping chasm that divided the length of the room.

As the group approached, a length of stone slid smoothly across the vast divide, providing a pseudo-bridge for the group to cross. As they did, the mages of the group flung their hands out into the air, setting magical traps that hovered above the entrance, while the rogues fashioned more traditional traps along the ground.

When the man in blue finally reached the other side, he stopped and looked around. Before him was a set of stairs, with three doors standing in a line at the top. As he made his way to the stairs, however, he found two of the three doors blocked by rubble.

"Set up a barrier on the stairway and prepare for combat. I'm certain the Beastmaster is with them, so brace yourselves for his horde. I'll return as soon as I can." ordered the man in blue.

As their leader disappeared up the staircase, the remainder of the group snapped into action – pulling out all the stops to try and delay their enemies as best they could. Every one of them was more concerned with the man in blue's quest than their own lives.

The archers and mages moved to the top of the stairs, leaving behind a multi-tiered defence barrier at the base, with a smaller barrier between the companions and the bridge.

It wasn't long until the doors burst open, and a horde of beasts began flooding the room. Several gave guttural yelps as they reached the traps set up around the perimeter. But the traps barely slowed them – overwhelmed by sheer numbers. One of the mages having spent the whole time chanting a single spell finally released it. The spell swept the bridge clear of monsters for a scant few seconds before more monsters flooded the bridge once again. The mage dropped to his knees in exhaustion before removing a potion from a pouch on his side, once finished, he rose to his feet refocusing on the battle before him.

Whole packs of wargs, demon bats and dire-bears stampeded toward the companions. Spells and arrows flew in an arc toward the oncoming mass, dropping several of the flying creatures out of the air, and wounding several of the beasts on the ground.

The front row of warriors held no weapons – locking their shields side-by-side to form a barricade to slow the rush enough for the rest of the group to whittle down the numbers with their weapons. The demon bats flew over the warriors, rushing the archers and mages ahead and killing many, before they were taken out.

Hearing the battle raging below, the man in blue turned back to help his friends.

Half of the companions' bodies were scattered across the temple ground, surrounded by the lifeless forms of beasts many times their numbers. The room was silent, except for the heavy breathing of the survivors.

They each looked towards the door in grim apprehension as the five warriors they had seen on the cliffs entered the temple. The five men strode in with imposing confidence, advancing leisurely across the bridge, before picking up speed as they approached the companions.

The five slaughtered the companions easily, their overwhelming power and strength seeming to create an aura that crackled between them. Within moments, the warriors were all dead, and the five advanced toward the stairs. As they reached the first barrier, one of them stepped forward. Their sword glowed with a bright golden sheen as it swung in a smooth arc, emitting a wave of light that shattered directly through the layers of the barrier.

As the last layer was destroyed, the man in blue stepped back into the room, pale-faced and horrified. Shock quickly turned to rage as his eyes fell upon the indifferent faces of his long-time enemies. In his fury, his whole body started to take on a slight glow, eyes blowing out to pitch black, and, in their depths, five points of coloured light shone through.

The man in blue cast a barrier of his own, thrusting a hand forward to reveal a small red orb, which slowly rose to float above his head. He repeated the gesture until five similar orbs were circling above him – red, green, blue, brown, and black.

In the space of a few seconds, the five orbs were sucked back down again, inside his body, and the glowing aura around him began to intensify.

He turned his head toward the hallway from where he had initially come, looking at the opening with an almost wistful expression. "The last orb was all I needed. I'm sorry I wasn't strong enough to save you all," he said.

He looked back at his enemies, who had destroyed his barrier and were closing in rapidly. The glow began to intensify to the point where the light was too bright to see his face anymore, and his expression of fury twisted into a feral grin of triumph.

An instant later, the power he had been channelling through the orbs exploded out in a flash of white, expanding across the stairs and upper floor in a moment, killing the last living souls in the room, including himself.

As the light faded, all that remained were pieces of flayed bone and shattered armour.

<u>Chapter 1</u>

The final image of the damaged temple and the former group was paused on a computer screen, three boys sat, staring at the remains.

Jasper Trico turned to his friends with a look of awe on his face. "How did you guys even know about this? That gameplay trailer was awesome," he whispered enthusiastically to his two best friends, Karl and Jono. The whispering was because they were in class, and they shouldn't have even been using the computer while the teacher was giving a lecture. But, since it was their last class of the day, they weren't exactly motivated to pay much attention.

"Maybe if you actually paid attention to what was coming out, you would have heard about Ariair Online before now. They have been teasing it for six months. Besides, we didn't say anything because we knew you were too busy trying to get everything in that MMO you have been playing on and off for, like, years now," declared Jono.

"And you have to buy the VR headset, which is pretty expensive. My parents bought it for me for my birthday last month. You need to come play with us; it just won't be the same if you aren't there competing against us. We plan to start as different races and on different continents and meet in this massive continent in the middle," added Karl.

"Fine. How much does the VR Helmet and game cost? And when do the servers go live?" Jasper responded, half in defeat.

Karl and Jono grinned at each other, knowing they had Jasper hooked. "They announced last week that the servers go live tomorrow night. We pre-ordered the game, so we're picking it up tonight, along with the headset. Though, for the game and headset, it costs about a grand, which was on special," Karl told Jasper.

"Do you boys have anything to add to my lecture on the use of strategy during World War II?" The boys all jumped at the voice of their teacher, Mr Gregory, who stared at them all with a profoundly unimpressed look.

"No, sir."

"Nope."

"Not a clue."

*

"Holy shit am I glad to be out of there! I swear, I almost had to start slapping myself in the face to stay awake in there," Karl declared, as the boys left class after another twenty minutes of being bored out of their minds under the hawk-like watch of Mr Gregory.

Jasper had never understood why Karl and Jono were such good friends. Karl was the typical archetype of a high school jock: slightly over 6 feet tall, with blonde hair and blue eyes, and a loud, boisterous personality that served him well as the school's star athlete. Jono, on the other hand, could only be described as a mousy guy: short, brown-haired, and brown-eyed, with a studious attitude, and fantastic grades.

Jasper considered himself to be somewhere in the middle: average height and build, with dirty blonde hair, and green eyes.

The three of them had been friends since the moment they met. Even though they were completely different people now, it had never had any effect on their relationship.

"Later guys! I have to work tonight. And, before you try and rant at me again, Jono, I will stop by the game store across from work before my shift to look at your damn game, okay?" Jasper chuckled as he walked away.

"See ya, man."

"You'd better," his friends shot back as they went the other way to drop their stuff back at their lockers.

*

After almost an hour switching buses, Jasper was almost at work. He always went straight to work from school though he was usually early since he didn't start until five. Considering he didn't like hanging around and he had promised his friends, he headed to the small shopping complex across the street from the supermarket, his workplace.

Entering the store, Jasper found a single employee playing a game on a small TV set up on the counter. He wore a bored expression. Looking around the store, Jasper thought it a little dingy, as if they didn't have a lot of customers.

"Hey, buddy. How's it going?" Jasper greeted the clerk.

Barely looking up from the game he was playing, the employee responded, "What can I do for you, my guy?"

"I was looking for a copy of Ariair Online, as well as the headset?" Jasper said, with a forced smile and jovial tone. Who would have thought that a year working in customer service would actually come in handy?

"Ha! Are you kidding me? That's been sold out for weeks, dude. Like, all the stock I have is for pre-orders," the clerk said wryly, before pausing thoughtfully. "Actually, you know what, I did get one extra that hasn't been reserved already. It's in a broken box, so I was just going to send it back to the suppliers, but I guess I could sell it to you instead," the clerk responded.

"As long as it isn't broken, I'll take it. Any chance of a discount, since it's in a broken box?" *And since you're an asshole,* he added silently.

"Nope. It's $1000, or I let someone else buy it. Take it or leave it. I don't care," replied the clerk with an uncaring smirk.

"Fine. I'll take it" Jasper said, teeth gritted.

The clerk walked into the back room for a few minutes and returned with a large box.

It had multiple warning labels, and a small amount of tape holding closed a rip on the side. It looked as though someone had purposefully torn it open to peek inside. The clerk also handed Jasper a clipboard with some paperwork on it and began speaking in a rehearsed manner.

"For legal purposes, we're required to get a signed waiver from all customers who wish to purchase the Ariair Online game and accompanying Virtual Reality headset. By committing to this purchase, you officially recognise that the Rustbel Company will not be liable for any mishaps, damage, injuries, etcetera, that may occur as a result of the headset's time compression technology. Consumers are also warned that excessive play may result in headaches and/or visual hallucinations, and that photosensitive epileptics are warned against gameplay, as flashing images and sounds may induce seizures – blah, blah, blah, blah… look, just sign the form and agree you won't sue them if you get fucked up while playing the game, okay?"

A master of skimming through the terms and conditions, Jasper read enough to gather the gist of what the paper said and signed where asked. He couldn't give less of a crap about big companies trying to cover their own asses – he just wanted to start to play the game as soon as possible. He hadn't been able to get the image of the trailer out of his head all day. Those five men mowing down the group of warriors; the shrieking beasts ripping the archers to shreds; the mage blowing himself up with the collection of orbs...

He couldn't wait to see what else he would find. The blurb on the box indicated that there were four starting countries with their individual native races. So intriguing, and he was excited to discover what they all were, and which ones he could choose to be.

Still fantasising about the adventures that lay ahead, he strolled back into work. For seven hours, he stared blankly into space, while occasionally serving the odd evening customer.

The only non-monotonous part of the night was when his attractive co-worker, Beth, came and began talking to him about her day. Flirting with her was one of the more enjoyable parts of his job. Mid-height, with dark purple hair, and a tattoo of a heart on her hip, she was considered far more 'alternative' than himself but was secretly just as much of a nerd as he was. Apparently, she hadn't heard of Ariair Online either, so they spent some time talking about the game.

*

After walking his co-worker to her car, Jasper waited for his mother to come pick him up since it was after midnight. Plagued with obsessive thoughts about the game, he grew more and more impatient the longer he had to wait – picturing himself setting the console up and beginning the game download over and over in his mind.

"Hey, honey!" his mother greeted him as she finally pulled up a few minutes later. "How was your day? What's with the big box?" she asked, peering at where he'd set the box and his backpack in the back seat in her rear-view mirror.

"Hey, ma. Thanks for picking me up again," Jasper responded, getting into the front and buckling his seatbelt. "You know, same old – only slept through three classes, and remarkably didn't get yelled at too much by customers. I, uh, might have spent some of my savings today on a new game. That's what's in the box. Brand new virtual reality set." Jasper slipped into his seat self-consciously, knowing his mother disapproved of his gaming. She saw it as a waste of valuable time that could be spent doing 'something productive.'

"Another one? Really? I thought you were saving up for a car?" she said, voice rising in anger. "I'm very disappointed in you, Jasper. You already waste too much time and money on those stupid games."

Struggling to find the words to satisfy her, he shifted for a second. "I know. But this one is different. The VR headset is equipped with this new technology called 'time compression', which basically means that **the game runs four times faster than real life** while being perceived as if in real-time. Theoretically, I could do my studying in the game, and have it done in a quarter of the time," he smiled at her his most magnificent winning grin. She didn't buy it.

The fifteen-minute drive home became very silent, and a little tense – his mother still quietly fuming next to him. Jasper barely moved, frozen like a deer in headlights. Once they arrived home, Jasper grabbed his stuff and ran straight into his room to unpack the box.

He placed it on his bed and began eagerly pulling the Styrofoam cube out of its box, easing one of the sides off to reveal the smooth exterior of the helmet. The outside had little else but a single button and a charging cable port, and the inside held a lot of sensors that were entirely beyond him.

The next thing in the box was a plain black power-supply box that plugged one cord into his computer and a power cable into the wall. After reading the instructions, he found that the helmet was wireless – he just needed to charge it every forty-eight hours of use. The box would come up on his computer as a program to download and grant him access to forums, auctions, etc.

After setting everything up, Jasper opened the program and started the download. Once it was finished, he could do his character creation before the servers started at 4pm local time. Seeing the updated information for the download, Jasper sighed in frustration when he saw that it was going to take over twelve hours.

“Slow, piece of shit computer,” Jasper muttered to himself.

It was with some reluctance that he resigned himself to get ready for bed, thinking that it could be worse. The headset ran off of the internet, instead of through the computer so it wouldn't be an issue after tonight. And when he woke up, he'd have all day to play his amazing new game.

Chapter 2: Character Selection

The next morning, Jasper sprung awoke with an enthusiasm that would have been entirely out of character on any other morning. He hoped that he'd been asleep long enough for the download to have finished.

Jasper moved to his computer, but what he saw caused his mood to quickly sour. "Four more hours... Are you kidding me?" he glared at his computer in betrayal for a moment, before tasking himself to get dressed in a pair of sweatpants quickly, and the first vaguely clean-smelling t-shirt he could find on the floor. Checking the time as he got dressed, he saw that it was only around nine in the morning, so he left his room and walked into the kitchen to make himself some breakfast.

His mother was in the kitchen, cleaning when he entered the room. "Morning. Where's dad?"

She turned around looking at him with a visibly annoyed expression. He assumed that she was still angry at him for his heavy spending, but it could also be his dad again.

"He is at the office again," she sighed. "Get yourself some breakfast and get out of the kitchen."

He nodded and grimly got to work.

His father was a Forensic Accountant – a profession which ate up far too much time away from home and was a primary cause of tension in their family. Aside from long hours in the office, there were also long business trips interstate and overseas to visit clients and partners. His fathers job had been the cause of a lot of arguments between his parents, and so he often found himself avoiding their reunion altogether when his father had been away from home for a while.

Not wanting to put his mother in a worse mood, Jasper hastened to prepare a plate of toast and went to hide in the living room and watch TV until the game had finished downloading.

*

The pinging sound of a completed download caused Jasper's ears to prick up eagerly. Rushing to his computer desk, Jasper grinned at the little green arrow signifying a successful installation.

Jasper followed the guide carefully, unplugging the fully-charged helmet from its box, and moving over to lie down on his bed. Jasper took a deep breath and hoped for the best before he reached up and slid the helmet over his eyes. The lack of sight weirded Jasper out for a moment, before a beep was heard, and, after a short moment of vertigo, another beep.

After another few seconds, a feminine voice piped up, "Scanning Complete."

A grey void faded into existence around him. Jasper looked down in shock to see that he no longer had a body – just a slight, amorphous glow. Suddenly, a light flashed, and he blinked to see a beautiful woman standing before him.

Outrageously tall, with a heart-shaped face, and a body that was so inhumanly attractive, he doubted anyone could even remotely resemble her in real life. The woman wore a white toga, not unlike the classic paintings of Greek or Roman gods.

Jasper realised he was staring at her buxom chest, he averted his eyes sheepishly, in doing so he saw that he had a body again; clad in the same clothes that he was wearing in real life.

"Hey there, how's it going? Oh, uh, I mean – Greetings, traveller! Welcome to our land of Ariair! You have come from your world to uncover what has been lost to time. You have the choice of what you do with your second life here. I am here to help create the new body your soul will inhabit while in our world. My name is Auna, and I am the goddess of Fate. Your first decision is this: what race do you wish to become?"

Jasper wasn't sure what was happening, but he wanted to know as much as possible before making his decision. After a moment of floundering in thought, he replied, "well, uh, I'm not really sure. Can I... see a list of the options, maybe?"

She smiled. "Let me show you."

A blue screen appeared in front of him.

Human
Halfling
Barbarian
Wolfman
High elf
Sun Elf
Drow
Wood Elf
Vampire
Naga
Dhamphir
Draconian
Bearfolk
Snakemen
Catfolk

"Wow. Okay. There are some pretty cool options here. Can I see some more details?" Jasper asked after reading the list, getting very excited when he saw his favourite mythical race.

The goddess giggled. "Of course, you can young Traveller."

The screen blinked.

Human
Can be any class
+5% ability level speed
+10% experience from monsters
5 free stat points per level

Halfling
Strength takes 2x points to increase
+50% experience in Crafting
+50% stats from gear
+1 Dex, +1 Int and 3 free stat points per level

Barbarian
Restricted to Melee classes
+5% extra damage from 2H Weapons
Extra 15% health from Vitality
+1 Str, +1 End and 3 free stats per level

Wolfman
+2.5% (Max. 15%) to all stats for every additional Wolfman in party
+20% Damage when unarmed
Locked to melee classes
+1 Str and 4 free stat points per level

"Human, or human-like. Fairly customizable, but has been pretty overdone," Jasper mused.

"These are the Races that start on the Island Kingdom of Leighest," the goddess explained.

"Leighest?" Jasper asked.

"All in good time, young one. Next are the inhabitants of Undris," replied the goddess, in a calmer tone than before.

Sun Elves
Light spells -50% Mana cost
Dark Spells +50% Mana cost
+15% Fire Resistance
+1 Int, +1 Wis, +1 Vit and 2 free stat points per level

The Drow
Dark Spells -50% Mana cost
Light Spells +50% Mana Cost
Dark Vision
+1 Int, +1 Wis and 3 Free stat points per level

High Elves
+35% Mana Regen speed
+15% Mana from Int
-5% Magic Resistance
+1 Int, +1 Agi and 3 free stat point per level

Wood Elves
+5% Movement increase in Forests
+1 Agi per every 2 levels
+50% Faster ability level with bows

+1 Dex, +1 Agi and 3 free stat points per level

"I've always liked elves, but I don't know if I really feel like it this time. Let's get to the more fun, monster-like races," Jasper requested.

Auna smirked at the hasty young man. "Fine then. If that's what you want, I will display the rest of the races without telling you anything about their Kingdoms."

Vampire
*+30% to all stats at night or in caves
-25% stats during the day.
Night Vision
+1 Agi, +1 End and 3 free stat points per level*

Dhamphir
*Gains 15% to all stats at night or in caves
Lose 5% stats during the day
Night Vision
+1 Str, +1 Agi, +1 End and 2 free stat points per level*

Naga
*Ignores water movement restriction
Breathe underwater
+20% Magic Resistance
+1 Agi, +1 Wis and 3 free stat points per level*

Bearfolk
+1 Str every 2 levels
+20% Physical Damage Resistance
-10% Mana cost of earth Magic
+1 End, +1 Vit and 3 free stat point per level

Snakefolk
+25% Regen Speed
+10% Movement speed in warm regions
-10% Movement speed in tundra regions
+1 Vit, +1 Agi and 3 free stat points per level

Catfolk
+1 Agi per 2 levels
+20% damage when unarmed
Night Vision
+1 Agi, +1 Dex and 3 free stat points per level

Draconian
Fall damage negated when gliding using wings
-50% mana cost for chosen affinity
+50% mana cost for opposing affinity
+1 Str +1 Int +1 Vit and 2 free stat points per Level

Jasper studied the different races for a moment each, before stopping on the final option, barely hearing Auna speak moments later.

"These are all of your options. Choose wisely," Auna said.

"Oh, hell yeah! Dragons!" Jasper caught himself and cleared his throat. "Uh, I mean, the Draconian race is the one I choose," he said, dialling his enthusiasm down to a far more acceptable level.

"Good. Now, you must choose a class to grow into. These are your options," Auna continued.

Elemental Mage
Light Armour Proficiency
Staff/Stave Proficiency or Wand Proficiency
**Elemental Magic Proficiency*
Choose Two:
Fire Bolt
Water Bolt
Wind Bolt
Earth Bolt
+1 Int and +1 Wis per level

Necromancer
Light Armour Proficiency
Staff/Stave Proficiency or Wand Proficiency
Dark Magic Proficiency
Choose Two:
Raise Undead
Dark Bolt
Curse of Affliction
Life Steal
+1 Int and +1 Wis per level

Druid
Light Armour Proficiency
Staff/Stave Proficiency or Wand Proficiency
Nature Magic Proficiency
Choose Two:
Rejuvenation
Beast Form
Earth bolt
Root Prison
+1 Int and +1 Wis per level

Shaman
Light Armour Proficiency
Staff/Stave Proficiency or Wand Proficiency
Earth Magic Proficiency
Choose Two:
Summon Totem
Earth Bolt
Summon Spirit Animal
Mana Leech
+1 Int and +1 Wis per level

Beastmaster
Medium Armour Proficiency
1H Weapon Proficiency
Dual Wield Proficiency
Choose Two:
Beast Tame
Inner Beast
Beast Sight
Beast Assimilation
+1 Str and +1 Int per Level

Summoner
Light Armour Proficiency
Staff/Stave Proficiency or Wand Proficiency
Dark Magic Proficiency
Choose Two:
Summon Familiar
Dark Bolt
Withering Curse
Blood Drain
+1 Int and +1 Wis per Level

Monk
Medium Armour Proficiency
Unarmed Proficiency
Light Magic Proficiency
Choose Two:
Restoration
Swift Strike
Jab
Meditate
+1 Str and +1 End per Level

Priest
Light Armour Proficiency
Staff/Stave Proficiency or Wand Proficiency
Light Magic Proficiency
Choose Two:
Slow Heal
Cure Poison
Holy Strike
Light Barrier

+1 Int and +1 Wis per Level

Scout
Medium Armour Proficiency
Bow Proficiency
Throwing Weapon Proficiency
1H Weapon Proficiency
Choose Two:
Stealth
Power Shot
Eagle Eye
Tracking
+1 Agi and +1 Dex per Level

Spellbow
Medium Armour Proficiency
Bow Proficiency
1H Weapon Proficiency
Throwing Weapon Proficiency
**Elemental Magic Proficiency*
Choose Two:
Power Shot
Fire Shot
Air Shot
Flash Shot
+1 Dex and +1 Int per Level

Hunter
Medium Armour Proficiency
1H Weapon Proficiency
Throwing Weapon Proficiency
Bow Proficiency

Dual Wield Proficiency
Choose Two:
Summon Pet
Power Shot
Flurry Strike
Tracking
+1 Dex and +1 End per Level

Ranger
Medium Armour Proficiency
1H Weapon Proficiency
Throwing Weapon Proficiency
Bow Proficiency
Dual Wield Proficiency
Choose Two:
Snipe Shot
Concealment
Concussive Shot
Tracking
+1 Agi and +1 Dex per Level

Thief
Medium Armour Proficiency
1H Weapon Proficiency
Thrown Weapons Proficiency
Dual Wield Proficiency
Choose Two:
Backstab
Stealth
Pickpocket
Lockpicking
+1 Dex and +1 Agi per Level

NightBlade
Medium Armour Proficiency
1H Weapon Proficiency
Thrown Weapon Proficiency
Dark Magic Proficiency
Dual Wield Proficiency
Choose Two:
Stealth
Dark Strike
Dark Bolt
Backstab
+1 Dex and +1 Int per Level

Assassin
Medium Armour Proficiency
1H Weapon Proficiency
Thrown Weapons Proficiency
Poison Proficiency
Bow Proficiency
Choose Two:
Poison Weapon
Stealth
Kill Strike
Stun Shot
+1 Dex and +1 Agi per Level

Bandit
Medium Armour Proficiency
1H Weapon Proficiency
Throwing Weapon Proficiency
2H Weapon Proficiency

Choose Two:
Mug
Pickpocket
Flurry Strike
Heavy Strike
+1 Str and +1 Dex per Level

Fighter
Medium Armour Proficiency or
Heavy Armour Proficiency
Shield Proficiency
1H Weapon Proficiency
2H Weapon Proficiency
Dual-Wield Proficiency
Choose Two:
Shield Bash
Heavy Strike
Flurry Strike
Iron Hide
+1 Str and +1 Vit per Level

Berserker
Medium Armour Proficiency or
Heavy Armour Proficiency
2H Weapon Proficiency
Rage Stat added
Choose Two:
Heavy Strike
Blood Rage
Merciless Kick
Frenzy Strike
+1 Str and +1 End per Level

Elemental Knight
Heavy Armour Proficiency
Shield Proficiency
1H Weapon Proficiency
2H Weapon Proficiency
Choose Two:
(Choice of) Affinity Strike
Shield Bash
Heavy Strike
+1 Str and +1 Int per Level

Paladin
Heavy Armour Proficiency
Shield Proficiency
1H Weapon Proficiency
2H Weapon Proficiency
Choose Two:
Heavy Strike
Shield Bash
Light Bolt
Light Heal
Holy Strike
Holy Aura
+1 Str and +1 Int per Level

"That's a good amount of options. Let's see – remove everything non-magic hybrid. What does that leave?" Jasper asked

A shorter simpler, list appeared in front of him.

Elemental Knight
Paladin
Nightblade
Spellbow
Monk

Meanwhile, Auna conjured herself a seat and sat down behind Jasper, outside his line of vision. She wasn't supposed to be seen sitting down, but she liked to do so when waiting for players to hurry up and make their decisions. She was uncertain whether or not he was even aware he'd been talking to himself out loud. After some time, when he finally turned back to her, she quickly stood back up and made the chair disappear again.

After twenty minutes of careful deliberation, weighing each option out in his mind, Jasper finally decided.

"They all sound interesting, but I keep changing my mind on what role I want to play. I've always been better as a damage dealer, but I make an alright healer, or Tank, as well. You know what? I think I'll go for the Elemental Knight. That way I can be either a Tank or a DPS." he said, referring to Damage per Second.

"So, you have chosen. One of the details that wasn't heavily detailed in the information is that the Draconian race each have an affinity that influences their inherent magic, as well as their looks. Here is the list of affinities. Just so you know, you will struggle to learn any magic from the opposite affinity," replied Auna.

Once again, the blue screen popped up, showing him a list.

Fire
Water
Wind
Earth
Light
Dark

"I assume the base affinity includes the ability to either gain more power or use less mana for any of the subsets of that base affinity? Like, Wind with Lightning, or Dark with Void. But I always liked the Crowd Control options and piercing effects of Ice magic, so I think I will go with Water as my affinity. To go along with that, I guess I still have to choose my abilities. To go with my chosen affinity, I choose Water Blade, and Heavy Strike," Jasper mused aloud, answering Auna.

Once Jasper had made his decision, an image of a dark blue draconian appeared before him. It was around his height, and reasonably slender. To the side of the image was a range of sliders to alter the character's size, build, colour, and wingspan. Jasper played with these options for a while until he was satisfied. The final product ended up being slightly bulkier, with darker blue scales, and a conservative wingspan.

"Alright, I'm done editing the body. Tell me more about the Kingdom that the Draconians live in?" Jasper asked as he turned back to Auna.

"Oh, yeah, of course." She cleared her throat. "The Kingdom of Dracon is home to Draconians, Bearfolk, Catfolk, and Snakemen. To the north of the island is the City of Cindera – it is close to a range of Volcanoes that are said to be the home of the progenitor of the Draconian race. Cindera is also the Capital, and home of the king. In the very south is the Keep of Draconia – originally built to keep away invaders and has become a trading hub since. You will be starting in River City, in the middle of the Kingdom. If you wish to know more, you need to find out on your own," Auna replied.

"Alright. Is that everything? Can I enter the world now?" Jasper said.

"Almost. Before you enter, you should also know that the currency used across the world is gold, silver, and copper. One hundred copper to one silver; one hundred silver to one gold."

He waited for her to continue speaking, allowing her to expand any more detail. When she stopped, he inclined his head expectantly. "Great. Okay. Is that all I need to know?"

Auna gave a cryptic smile and nodded. "Good luck on your journey. I daresay you'll need it," she laughed. "Have fun…"

And with that, before Jasper could say another word, Auna disappeared, and the world went dark. Before he could even register the change, he felt himself falling once more.

Chapter 3

A large market square faded into view before Jasper.

At the centre of the hub, a large fountain acted as the centremost point of the crossroads between four different cobblestone streets. The right-most path led to a gate, guarded by a small group of bored-looking soldiers. In every other direction, the streets were lined with buildings.

Peering up to get a better look at the fountain, Jasper inspected the imposing stone figure of a proud-looking Draconian, who wore heavy armour and a severe expression. A bronze plaque below the statue informed him that the being was named General Douga, and he was celebrated as the Saviour of River City.

Jasper assumed he'd probably either have to go to a library or ask someone about the fountain to get any real detail about it. He liked worlds with lore but wasn't all that interested in finding out about the statue.

For the first time, Jasper finally thought to look down at his body and saw that he was wearing a plain cotton tunic, cotton pants and simple leather boots. With a thoughtful noise, Jasper started to walk down the nearest street, only to fall face-first on the ground, almost immediately.

5 damage received

Jasper braced a hand on the fountain to stand back up and attempted to not trip over his tail again. He felt the strain of using muscles that he didn't have in his regular body. For the next ten minutes, he allowed himself time to flex his wings and sweep his tail from side-to-side, getting used to the foreign appendages, and adjusting his centre of gravity to compensate the imbalance.

"Well, shit. I didn't expect to have pretty much to re-learn how to walk. This place sure smells like what I assume a medieval village smelled like. Without the exposed sewers, though, I guess," Jasper thought to himself.

Cautiously this time, Jasper began to walk down the street to his right toward the guarded gate. Behind the wall fringing the path, he could hear the muffled sounds of yelling voices and the clashing of weapons. He thought it safe to assume that it was some sort of training grounds. Next to the gate, another opening in the wall was blocked off by a group of guards. Peering through, Jasper could see wagons unloading foodstuffs into a building, and an open field, where many young-looking people of multiple races were sparring amongst themselves.

Upon reaching the gate, Jasper saw a Draconian guard standing to his right. A massive example of the race, the guard stood a good half-foot taller than him and was a deep reddish-black colour. The guard radiated authority. He wore what Jasper assumed was the standard heavy armour for guards, as it matched the ones of the guards by the training area – silver, with a crest on the breast that resembled two swords crossed in front of a kite shield, much like the broadsword and shield the guard himself was equipped with.

Jasper approached him, hoping for a tutorial quest, such as parcel delivery, or killing some low-risk wildlife.

"Greetings, Sir guard. I am a new adventurer in town and was hoping for some advice. Or, if you could use some help, I've come to offer my assistance." Putting on his best 'pity me' expression, Jasper hoped to convince the man to help him.

"Hello. You sure do seem young. Are you sure you're an adventurer? You seem awfully under-equipped to do anything that I need to be done. Actually, if you feel like heading back into town proper, I have a delivery that got dropped off here by a merchant that needs to go to the Barracks Blacksmith," the guard exposed helpfully.

Truthfully, Jasper had always enjoyed mini-games involving making, repairing, or upgrading his own weapons but he felt this game might work a little different. When playing characters with heavy armour, he had a tendency to learn blacksmithing, mining, and enchanting – he hoped he'd be able to convince the blacksmith to teach him a repair ability, at least.

Ecstatic to have his first quest, Jasper grinned excitedly. "I'd be happy to do that for you, Sir."

Immediately, a blue screen appeared in front of him.

Quest Accepted! - Delivering Supplies
You have agreed to deliver a package to the River City Guards Blacksmith for Guard Captain Kieras
Reward:
Further interaction with the Gate Guards of River City

"Man, I learnt a fair amount just from the Quest screen," muttered Jasper after reading the window.

"What was that, boy?" asked Captain Kieras. He handed Jasper a large crate, removed from his Inventory.

"Nothing, just talking to myself," Jasper responded with a smile. Grunting with effort, he picked up the crate and began walking back down the street, towards the opening in the wall that was guarded. He assumed the building there was the barracks.

Less than halfway there, Jasper's legs began to wobble under the strain of the cargo's weight, and he took a brief pause to catch his breath, sitting on the crate. After a few minutes rest to gather his bearings once more, he continued on his way, arms burning as he heaved the package along with him. The guards at the entrance stopped him for an explanation, but quick name-dropping of Captain Kieras allowed him through.

Once again out of breath and sore, he finally got around the side of the building and saw the entrance to the Blacksmith. Just inside the door, a hulking Bearfolk wearing a leather smock was hammering on a piece of Iron.

"Excuse me, I have a package for you," Jasper said as he hesitantly entered the forge area. The Blacksmith looked up at him for a second, before ignoring him, and returning to work on finishing what appeared to be a set of pauldrons. Eventually, he brought his goggles to the top of his head, ceased his hammering, and looked at Jasper.

"Well then, bring it over here, lad."

As soon as Jasper put the crate on the bench before him, the lid was quickly ripped off by the Blacksmith.

"Ahh, the silver ore I have been waiting for. I'm fixing the Captain's armour with it – what did he promise you as a reward for doing this?"

"Well, he actually didn't specify a reward, I was just kinda hoping you could teach me a thing or two?"

The Blacksmith started laughing. "A little runt like you? You're exhausted just from carrying this box from the gate; you really think you can become a blacksmith? You know what, I'm feeling generous. If you can get to level ten and bring me fifty pieces of ore you have mined yourself, I will teach you how to be a Blacksmith."

A couple of screens popped up, but he swiped them away, deciding he would check them later.

"Thank you, but, actually I just want to be able to repair my gear while out adventuring. I don't have the time I would need to dedicate to become a true Blacksmith. And I don't have a Mining skill or a pickaxe, either."

The blacksmith stroked his chin thoughtfully. "Well, I suppose I can give you the skill book to teach you Mining, and once you bring back the ore, I can give you the Repair skill book. I have a pickaxe I can sell you for two silver, no problem."

Jasper called up his inventory, realising that he didn't even know how much starting funds he had.

Simple wooden buckler
Basic Broadsword
Bronze Plate Armour Set
10 hard bread
5 waterskins
25S

Realising he was an idiot for not checking earlier, he eagerly agreed. A pickaxe was handed to him, and he stowed it away in his inventory.

A pop-up icon to the bottom left of his vision flashed again, and he figured that, when he flicked a notification away, it merely minimised into the corner. Curious, he brought them up.

Quest Completed! – Delivering Supplies
You have delivered the crate of Silver Ore for Captain Kieras
Reward:
50 Exp
Mining Skill Book

Quest Accepted! - Blacksmith's Request
The blacksmith Coal has agreed to teach you to repair
Equipment
Requirements:
Level 10
50 Pieces of Ore

Reward:
Repair Skill Book

Congratulations!
*For repeatedly pushing your body to the limits of your stamina,
you have earned:*
+2 Str
+2 End

Jasper quickly used the Mining skill book.

Skill Learnt:
Mining Beginner level 1
Get into the dirt and start digging for ore.

"Damn, not bad for a single delivery quest," Jasper noted, impressed. "Status," he added, and another box came up.

Status
Name: *None*
Alignment: *Neutral*
Level: *1*   **Exp:** *60/100*
Class: *Elemental Knight*
Race: *Water Draconian*
Money: *23S*   **Gender:** *Male*
Title: *None*
Fame: *0*   **Infamy:** *0*
-

Health: *100/100*   **Health Regen:** *0.05/Sec*
Mana: *100/100*   **Mana Regen:** *0.05/Sec*
Stamina: *100/100*   **Stamina Regen:** *1.0/Sec*

Strength: 12   *Dexterity: 10*
Agility: 10   *Endurance: 12*
Vitality: 10   *Intelligence: 10*
Wisdom: 10   *Luck: 10*

Affinity:
Water

Abilities:
Water Strike Beginner Level 1
Heavy Strike Beginner Level 1

Skills:
Mining Beginner Level 1

Upon seeing his Status page, Jasper realised he had never specified his name, and quickly added his name down as Ishtar. He had always used that name for characters, even though he still got teased by his friends for naming his character after a goddess.

Wanting to get some real experience in the game, Ishtar headed back to the Captain, looking for another quest to get increase in his experience.

"Captain," he greeted. "The package has been delivered. Are there any other quests available? Maybe some low-level beast that needs to be exterminated?"

"And what is the name of such a 'heroic' adventurer that comes to the guards, instead of going off to find the adventurer's guild, hm?"

"Ishtar, Captain," he replied.

The captain laughed derisively. "Alright. Just this once, I will give you the quest. But, next time, you need to go off and find the guild to get these quests yourself, you hear? There is a need to thin out the numbers on the Horned Rabbits in the fields outside town. You do that; you'll get a nice little reward."

"Thank you, Captain."

Quest Accepted! - Thin the Herd
You have been tasked to kill 15 Horned Rabbits
Reward:
75 Exp
25C

Ishtar headed out the gate and kept walking until he came across a field laden with twitchy-nosed Horned Rabbits. They looked like regular wild rabbits, except for a white spiralled horn attached to their heads.

He quickly looked at the stats of his sword and shield as he equipped them.

Basic Broadsword
Type: *Broadsword* **Durability:** *30/30*
Quality: *Basic* **Damage:** *1-5*
A very basic bronze Broadsword

Simple Wooden Buckler
Type: *Shield* **Durability:** *30/30*
Quality: *Basic* **Defence:** *15*
A plank of wood with a handle

They were pretty much par for the course in terms of starter gear: crappy weaponry, but with surprisingly generous defence on the buckler.

Ishtar walked towards the first Horned Rabbit he found. It placidly ate grass and paid no attention to him until he was within striking distance of it. It then froze, ducking its little head down a little, seeming guarded. Lifting the buckler and sword into a position that felt about right, Ishtar crept towards it.

Suddenly, it leapt at him. Piercing a gap in the armour on his leg, it speared him through the thigh with a pointed horn.

Received 15 Damage

Ishtar cried out in agony, not ready for that level of pain. Quickly attempting to hit the rabbit back, he swung the sword as it dodged past him, missing entirely. Ishtar set himself into an offensive stance before the rabbit could jump at him again, and he stabbed his sword at it, just barely hitting it as it leapt out of the way.

Dealt 10 Damage

A red health bar appeared above the rabbit, half the colour in it empty. Distracted by the bar, he didn't notice as the rabbit dove for him once again, this time, hitting him square in the chest, and penetrating right through his bronze armour.

Critical Hit!
Received 45 Damage

With half his health gone, Ishtar gritted his teeth in frustration at how he was literally losing to the weakest creature in the game. This time, when the rabbit dove at him again, he swung his shield up to cover himself, and the rabbit bounced off, hitting the ground in a daze.

Ishtar stabbed it again before it could get back up, finally killing it.

You have successfully killed:
Horned Rabbit x1
You have gained 10 Exp

Happy about his first kill, Ishtar bent down to touch the body, hoping for a loot menu. To his delight, a new window appeared in front of him.

__Loot Menu__
Horned Rabbit Horn
Rabbit Fur
2C
Take all Yes/No

Quickly hitting Yes, Ishtar looked around to find his next victim.

Chapter 4: The Next Step

Having killed ten of the fifteen Horned Rabbits he needed for the quest, Ishtar was now at level two. He'd gained two free stat points but didn't use them immediately, hoping to get a few extra free stat points by completing tasks like his delivery of the crate earlier.

He had also used up a lot of his food and water for healing benefits. Spying another Horned Rabbit, he eagerly crept towards it. There were four others nearby, so he figured that he could pretty much finish the quest straight away.

Having noticed the pattern of the attacks, it took very little time to kill the first two individually, until the last two attacked him at the same time, each from different directions. Taken by surprise, he took both hits.

Received 10 Damage

Received 10 Damage

Ishtar recovered quickly and attacked the closest with his new ability.

"WATER STRIKE."

His sword began to glow a bright, luminescent blue. The colour seemed to deepen for a moment as if charging, and once it had stopped, it started to undulate like an ocean current. He quickly stabbed his sword towards the first one, killing the rabbit with a single strike.

Shaking his head at his own stupidity for not using either of his abilities before now, Ishtar turned around to find the other Rabbit moving towards him, horn poised directly at him. He quickly lifted his shield to protect himself. Feeling the impact of the rabbit not long after, Ishtar decided to try his Heavy Strike ability.

"HEAVY STRIKE."

To his disgust, the rabbit didn't just die – it was pulverised. Immediately classifying that ability as overkill for the smaller prey, he made quick work of looting the Horned Rabbits.

> **You have successfully killed:**
> *Horned Rabbit x4*
> *You have gained 40 Exp*

Ishtar sat down to rest while he waited for his health, mana, and stamina to regenerate. He ate his second to last piece of bread and drank a little more water.

One more rabbit and he could go back into town to get his rewards and sell all the crap he'd accumulated that he didn't need. Counting up the meat portions in his inventory, he figured he could save money by cooking.

Hunting around for the last Horned Rabbit needed to finish the quest, Ishtar noticed that the light had been slowly fading to darkness for quite a while now without him noticing. Getting closer to the fringe of the woods in his search, he heard movement between the trees and slowed to a crawl, trying to sneak up on the final Horned Rabbit.

As he was getting nearer and nearer to the sound of dry leaves rustling and twigs snapping, Ishtar's scaly forehead furrowed in a frown. The noises suggested that, whatever was making those sounds, it was far too large to be another rabbit. He began to inch his way back the way he came, choosing caution over curiosity.

Long, quadrupedal forms moved out of the trees. Trying to focus hard on the creature as it stalked towards him, a screen appeared.

Congratulations!
You have discovered a Hidden Skill!
Appraisal Beginner Level 1
You can now identify information about items, monsters, and beasts that you don't own

Night Wolf
***Type:** Beast **Level:** 3*
These wolves only come out from their sleeping places at night, primarily using ambush tactics.

Very happy with his new skill, Ishtar quickly put it to good use by identifying the creature to glean any useful information.

"Oh, shit," he muttered, moving quickly.

Ishtar dashed towards the wolf and got ready to use an ability.

"HEAVY STRIKE."

Ishtar slashed his longsword towards the wolf, but the wild canine quickly squatted down and leapt to the side, swinging its claws at Ishtar as he went past. The swipe grazed his side, and did substantial damage, taking off about a third of his health.

Received 40 Damage

Reeling back from the hit, Ishtar saw the wolf leap toward him again. He quickly raised his shield in front of his upper body to defend himself and was sent flying backwards from the impact of the animal. Once waiting for the Wolf to leap toward him, he defensively lifted both his shield and sword. As it got closer to him, he prepared for his counter-attack.

"WATER STRIKE"

Ishtar dodged to the side as the Wolf leapt, and he managed to stab into its side as it sailed past. He made a noise of triumph as the sword landed near the heart, but that victorious shout quickly turned to a yelp of pain as he was wounded in the attempt.

CRITICAL HIT
Dealt 75 Damage

Received 25 Damage

A health bar appeared above the wolf after his successful strike. Ishtar saw that he had taken off the vast majority of the wolf's health with his successful attack. He considered this; while Heavy Strike was apparently the more effective of the two, it was also far slower than Water Strike – no good against a speedy enemy like this.

As the wolf leapt again Ishtar rolled away, ending up on his back near the feet of the dog. He raised his shield by instinct, but still felt the buckler shatter on impact with the wolf's head. Fortunately, the blow seemed to stun his opponent, and he took the opportunity to try again.

"HEAVY STRIKE!"

The attack landed.

CRITICAL STRIKE
Dealt 100 Damage

You have successfully killed:
Night Wolf x1
You have received 50 Exp

Panting from the effort, Ishtar quickly looted the wolf corpse and resolved to get the hell out of there before any more showed up. Yet, as he selected 'Yes' on the option to take all items, he found himself hit from the back by a substantial weight. He screamed in pain at the feeling of sharp teeth sinking into his neck, and the last thing he saw was two more Night Wolves before the world went blank.

YOU HAVE DIED
You have 24 hours before you are able to sign on again!
You have lost all skill and ability progress made since last level up!
As you are under level 10, you will not lose a level!

*

Jasper threw the helmet down in outrage as he stood up.

"Piece of shit. Where the hell did those wolves come from? Come on!" he raged, glancing around his empty room as if expecting someone to agree with him.

Angry that he couldn't log back in for another twenty-four hours, Jasper decided to leave home to go and hang out somewhere else instead. He tried to call both Jono and Karl but got no answer. He supposed they were both still playing.

He was still fuming half an hour later, glowering down at the street as he walked into the mall for something to do. He found himself obsessively arguing at the unfairness of such a feature inside his head. Losing experience after dying seemed fair enough, but not being able to log in for a full 24 hours? That had to be something they'll patch in a few weeks, right?

Eyes trained on the ground in front of him, Jasper's train of thought immediately derailed as he felt someone collide with him solidly. The impact sent Jasper sprawling to the ground. He looked up in a daze, an apology for his carelessness on the tip of his tongue. When his eyes lifted, he saw three people standing over him, glowering as though he'd just personally insulted each of their mothers in detail. The person he ran into stepped forward with a pissed look on his face.

"What's the big idea, you moron? Watch the hell where you're walking."

Jasper blinked in surprise at the unwarranted aggression, and the apology died on his lips. He scowled. "It was an accident, you asshole. I would've apologised if you'd given me a chance," with dignity, he picked himself off the ground and dusted off his jeans.

The guys appeared around his age – big, and beefy, with small craniums and wide jaws, though that could have been his imagination. The two lackeys, behind the one who had spoken, immediately stepped forward and pressed him back against the wall, holding a shoulder each in their meaty grips.

"Smartass little prick," the big one growled, stepping into his personal space with an ugly, twisted look on his face. "My father's on the board of Rustbel, do you know what that means? Means you need to learn a little respect."

Without giving Jasper a chance to say anything, the leader stepped away and allowed the two bigger lackeys to drag him into an alleyway between two shops. Jasper was promptly thrown to the ground, and the two guys turned to block him off from the exit. The leader advanced on him, and Jasper lunged forward before he could get the chance to strike first – throwing his fist out in a hard punch, which the guy easily dodged.

Undeterred, Jasper jabbed out quickly, again and again, only for the guy to sweep out of the way each time, a smug expression on his face growing meaner and haughtier with each failed swipe. He was mocking him.

Apparently tired of their dance, the guy set his feet, no longer dodging, and landed a powerful kick to the dead-centre of Jasper's chest before he had a chance to get out of the way. The blow sent Jasper's head cracking against the brick alleyway wall, and before he could even gather his bearings, the front of his shirt was balled up in the guy's fist and his shoulders were shoved back into the wall. A meaty fist sank into his stomach and Jasper doubled over, struggling to catch his breath.

The guy laid into him, throwing punch after punch into Jasper's torso. After taking a sharp blow to the head, the world began to swim, utterly disorientating him. The last thing he registered was the feeling of the big guy being ripped away from him, followed by the sounds of swift hits and grunting. When he opened his eyes again, the three teens were on the floor, writhing, each clutching different injured body parts.

An arm came around his back, supporting his weight gingerly as he was led out of the alleyway.

"C'mon, lad. Let's get you inside while their driver picks up those three cretins."

By the time Jasper came back to his senses, he found himself sitting upright in a small office, head in his hand. A cursory glance around the walls, and he deduced that he was in some kind of martial arts studio. Pictures of students in white uniforms lined the wall around the main desk, and assortments of wooden and metallic weapons were in displays up against the opposite wall.

A figure rounded the corner into the office – a half-Asian man, wearing a crisp, black martial arts uniform, carried a bottle of Powerade and an ice pack in either hand. He handed them both to Jasper.

"Thanks for the help," Jasper murmured, wincing as he pressed the ice pack to a tender spot on his head. "Who are you?"

"My name is Glen Yamoto. I am the master at this Dojo. How are you feeling?"

"Jasper Trico. I'm alright, I think my dignity took more of a beating than the rest of me," he winced as he adjusted, taking stock of his bruised ribs and swollen face. "Dunno what the hell those guys' problem was," he added in an unhappy mutter.

"I never liked those boys. But their fathers are quite rich, and I've never had a reason to ban them before today. I'm sorry you were attacked by my students, they behaved most dishonourably. Their aggression has worsened since they started raving about a new game. They were always arrogant, and have tried to act superior to others, but never to this extent," Glen said, regret creeping into his voice.

Jasper took a moment to review his surroundings, "This is a cool place," he said, "I had no idea this was here. What do you teach?"

Glen laughed. "My other instructor and I teach multiple forms of martial arts, but we are quite well-known for our United Weapon Masters coaching. UWM is live fighting with full body armour and metal weapons. We have a few different grades, as well as private lessons."

"That sounds awesome. That might be a great help, actually. Do you have any enrolment information?"

"Maybe. If you do join, the first thing you need to learn is not to let your anger get the better of you again. Control is an important thing here – we will not tolerate aggression or antagonisation. So, if you choose to start here, the first thing I will help you with is keeping calm through meditation."

Jasper and Glen continued to speak about meditating, and the basic training that is done at the dojo. It was some time of chatting before Jasper finally felt he had recovered enough to leave. He left with a book on meditation under his arm, and a hopeful outlook on what he would learn at the Dojo, how it would help him to not only defend himself in the future but in the game as well.

He was considering quitting his crappy job to try and make money from the game, but that was most likely a pipe dream. There were always lazy people or people who had too much money, who bought their gear from the auctions. With his chance of finding some decent gear that was useless to him, he could use the real money auctions. If the game had them that is.

In a much better mood than when he left home, Jasper headed back to the bus stop with a clear resolve to start reading the forums and find any other information he could to learn to play the game properly.

Chapter 5

Upon arriving home, Jasper started to read the book Glen had given him, intrigued by the concept and eager to learn more. The book wasn't very long, and he'd finished it in under an hour. Jasper was considering what to do next when he remembered his idea of reading through forums to get some more information about the game before he was able to log back on.

After browsing for several hours, Jasper was eventually satisfied with his knowledge regarding the in-game auction houses where they accepted either physical cash or game currency for any of the items. He just had to find one in any of the cities.

He learnt how his skills and abilities worked, and how there are five levels of everything: Beginner, Basic, Intermediate, Advanced and Master. At each level, the skills gave bonuses, and the abilities either changed or gained a significant increase in their power. He could get as many 'profession skills' as he wanted, but the forums advised picking a main few to really concentrate on.

Better yet, he learnt about the way the technology of the helmet worked.

The helmet induced a kind of artificial version of REM sleep – meaning that his body wouldn't move, so he was essentially playing while sleeping. Though, because the body still needs slow-wave deep sleep, it was advised that the game was only played for part of the night so that the user even got sufficient sleep. Finally, when his death message said twenty-four hours, it had actually meant in-game hours, so he only had a total of six hours once dead before he could get back into the game. Since he was killed around three hours before, he just had three left before he could log back in.

Thoughtfully, Jasper considered the possibility of a gaming marathon – logging off twice a day for his scheduled bathroom and food breaks – so that he could manage to get around four in-game days of training before having to go back to school on Monday. Judging by the slight increases in his stats when he'd carried the crates for delivery, hard training at a low level might net him a decent amount of extra stat points before he started levelling up again. He might even try to get some extra abilities or skills.

His plan, upon getting back into the game, was to continue exploring the city a bit more, which included trying to find the Adventurers Guild and the Mage Guild. He could even go back to the training field at the barracks he'd passed to see if they would train him, even though he wasn't a guard.

Still with a couple hours left before he could start playing again, Jasper went out to the kitchen to have some dinner with his family, attempting to try and appease his mother, who was still angry at him for buying the game.

As he entered the kitchen, he saw his mother finishing up dinner.

"Oh my God, what happened to your face?" his mother immediately demanded upon seeing him.

"Don't worry, mum. Some idiot knocked me down by accident, and I hit my head," Jasper lied smoothly.

"Oh, honey. Just sit down and have your dinner, and you can go to bed early tonight with some painkillers," his mother replied with a sympathetic look on her face. This worked out well in his favour, as that was his plan anyway.

*

Finally back in the game, Ishtar found himself in a pure white temple standing before a beautiful, white marble and gold fountain. Seeing a priest nearby, Ishtar approached him to find out about the god whose temple he had been resurrected in.

"Hello, Father. Can you tell me about this temple?" Ishtar inquired.

"Greetings, Traveller. Is this your first time resurrecting into one of the temples? If you're not a disciple of a particular God, you will resurrect into this temple: the home of Iplios, the goddess of life and nature, in the closest city," the Priest responded helpfully.

"Yes, Father. Since I am new to this world, I know very little about it, honestly. Is there any fee for the resurrection?" inquired Ishtar.

"There is no fee for the resurrection, but you may lose gold or items whenever you die. I can give you some more information about the Upper Pantheon if you wish? And, perhaps, request a donation towards the church to help the poor?" the priest added slyly.

"Sure," said Ishtar, handing over one of his silvers, before peering to see how much money he had left. 25S and 50C. He must have lost a bit, he wasn't keeping track as he killed the Rabbits.

"Iplios be with you, traveller. The Upper Pantheon consists of the goddess of fate, Auna; the god of death and darkness, Vames; the goddess of magic, Imera; the god of war and strategy, Ryter; the god of skills and knowledge, Uklena; and my goddess, Iplios – the goddess of life and nature. They all have lesser gods and powerful spirits under them, but we don't know much about most of them. You must be a disciple of our church to learn more. Is there anything else I can help you with?"

"No, thank you. I think I'm going to explore more of the city," responded Ishtar, as he walked towards the exit. Leaving the temple, Ishtar crossed a large garden that surrounded the building. Upon reaching the road, he looked around, seeing temples for all the other Upper Gods, each with their own colour scheme.

Unsure of where to go, Ishtar decided to let luck pick his route, and flipped a coin into the air. The bronze coin flew upward above his head, for a scant few seconds, before bouncing and rolling to Ishtar's right. He shrugged and bent down to pocket the coin before setting off in the rightward direction.

Part way down the street, Ishtar entered what looked like a town square, with a plain fountain in the centre, and market stalls selling a variety of different products. He was still unsure of where he was. Upon asking the closest merchant at the stall, he found that he was very close to the Adventurers Guild that Kieras had told him to check out the last time he was in town.

Arriving outside the Guild, Ishtar saw that the building was three stories tall with a pair of guards manning their post outside. He entered the building, walked up to the counter, and spoke to the woman who was seated behind.

"Hi, I wanted to register to be a part of the guild." Ishtar offered immediately, "I'm fine with starting at the lowest rank if I can finish this up quickly."

The woman reached under the desk and rummaged a hand around in one of her drawers, a neutral expression on her face. "Greetings. Yeah, you don't really have a choice about starting at the lowest rank. But, if you put your thumb on the corner of this status plate, we can get your details and register you as an F-Rank Adventurer."

Ishtar looked at the small grey metal plate that was handed to him. It was plain and blank before it was given to him, but after a stab of pain in his finger and a small drain on his mana, it started to change colour and fill with details. Ishtar watched a simple version of his stats appear on the, now brown, plate before showing it to the receptionist again. The woman paused for a moment to read through the details on the plate before continuing.

"Each time you upgrade your Adventurer rank, you will get a new colour-identifying status plate to make it easier to identify your rank within the Guild. The rankings in ascending order go F, Brown; E, Red; D, Blue; C, Green; B, Bronze; A, Silver; S, Gold; and SS, White. You will not find anyone above

A-Rank easily on this island – most head to the Lost Continent. There is a 5S fee for joining the Guild. Is there any additional information you require?" the receptionist scripted off in a clearly well-practised speech.

Quickly paying the fee, Ishtar asked, "Are there any good merchants nearby who I can buy some useful things for a beginner Adventurer from? And do you have any F-Rank quests that I can accept?"

"You are able to purchase items such as equipment, maps, and food from me here," responded the receptionist professionally.

Studying the gear Ishtar decided to forego buying any items, as they were really no better than his original starter gear. He bought a simple world map, a refill of his water skins, and a few days worth of food, before heading to where he hoped the training grounds near the west wall would be.

He took note of a mountain silhouette he could see near the border of a town, he knew he'd inevitably have to go there to get the Ore for Coal's quest.

Opening his map, which the game allowed him to rotate and zoom in on the city's details as well as his own location, he discovered himself to be on the north-west side of town, near the temple area on the north side. Just outside of town, on the map, a small skull mark was printed next to a copse of trees. Ishtar assumed that was where he had died. Though, at later levels, he would need to know where that was if he wanted to reclaim valuable dropped loot. Wanting to remember that place just in case he died again; he made a checkpoint on the map so that he could get some revenge on those damn wolves after he had levelled himself up.

Finding the main road heading south, he followed it to the original square he first appeared in and, once again, headed down a familiar road towards the training ground.

Entering the area, Ishtar saw that it was once again filled with young men and women doing many types of training under the tight control of their instructors. Those instructors were overseen by a Snakefolk woman, wearing dark leather, and positively decked out in swords, knives, and daggers holstered over her entire body. Every time Ishtar looked away from her, he started to forget what her exact details were, only able to remember that she was a Black Snakefolk. She was by far the most intimidating being in the area; the light seemed to fade as it approached her. Ishtar felt a cold sweat drip down the back of his neck when he tried to concentrate on her, he had never seen her before, but she scared the crap out of him.

He decided to try his new Appraisal ability on her.

Captain Quattra
Race: *Snakefolk* ***Level:*** *???*
Class: *Nightblade*

His appraisal didn't give him much information about Quattra, likely due to his own low level.

Ishtar walked up to her, hopeful that she would accept him. He really wasn't sure how many of the people here were NPCs and how many were actual players. Especially since he hadn't gone to the other side of town to see the other Guilds, having initially spawned near the Guards/Military quarter.

According to his map, the Keep was in the middle of town, with an offshoot of the river that gave the city its name being used as their moat. The Temple District to the North, The Adventurers Guild and the bazaar areas to the northeast side of town, the Guards and Military to the Southeast, Docks to the Northwest and the rest of the Guilds dominating the Southwest side of town. Ishtar still hadn't been west of the Keep, but he felt he probably should travel that way once he made a little more money.

Arriving in front of Quattra, Ishtar drew in a breath and projected as much confidence as he could muster. "Captain Quattra. Although I am an

Adventurer, instead of a guard, I'd like to request your permission to be trained in these grounds."

Quattra seemed confused by this. Using her own version of Appraisal, she pulled up the young Draconians stats and abilities, pondering what she could see of him.

"Weak," she eventually said, clipped and severe. "You are very weak. But I'm aware of the favour you performed for my dear lazy Captain, and so I will grant this request. I'll give you my special personal training for one week. 5S," she smirked, the expression sinister on a face like hers. The nearby eavesdropping instructors shuddered at her tone and shook their heads in pity for the poor unsuspecting bastard.

Quest Accepted! - Superior Training
You will be personally trained by the Training Grounds Captain.
Time Limit:
One Week worth of Training
Reward:
Increase of Stats and Proficiencies

Just a short time later, Ishtar realised just how much of a mistake he had made.

She started by having him do continuous push-ups at her feet, screaming in his face about how weak and pathetic he was. If he protested, she added more weight to his back. Following this, he was made to run around the entire perimeter of the grounds, glancing fervently around for her shadowy figure before she suddenly appeared in front of him, swinging a stick in his direction to catch him off-guard. He found himself eating food and drinking the extra potions she had given him in that training session just to keep his health up.

Ishtar stood with his sword and shield in hand, facing off against his instructor. Quattra easily deflected each of his sword blows as they came, and sliced shallow cuts into every limb with light, smooth movements as if mocking him. He was completely outclassed in skill. After reaching half-health, Quattra finally stopped him, a look of disgust on her face.

She dragged him over to a training dummy by his collar.

"Keep your shield up to cover your face, but not your eyes! Now, I'm going to show you some katas that I want you to follow. It will go diagonal slash, top to bottom from the right; same from left. Secondly: stab, stab, spin to increase force, and horizontal slash. Third: you will step forward, shield bash, downwards slash. These can also work for two-handed weapons. You will practice this non-stop for the next three hours."

So, practice for hours on end, Ishtar did.

By the time dusk was edging beyond the horizon, Ishtar could barely move for the deep pain in his every muscle. He was really regretting keeping the 60% pain settings he'd left it at.

Thinking back to the book he had read on meditating, he sat down next to the closest wall, crossing his legs. Trying to clear his mind seemed impossible and wasn't working. Considering the moves in the katas, he sank deeper into his mind, feeling the moves his body had been making. Having those moves ingrained into his mind had him seeing how he could incorporate the movements properly with his abilities.

Congratulations!
You have discovered a Hidden Skill!
Meditation Beginner Level 1
Speeds up mana and health recovery. Can slowly increase certain ability and skill levels if a breakthrough is achieved.

After he finished meditating, he saw that it was late at night, and decided that he should log off for a little bit to take care of bathroom and food breaks. As scheduled.

Chapter 6: Revenge

At the end of his week being trained by Quattra, Ishtar stumbled out of the training grounds with a nervous tick. He whipped his head around in a terrified manner, worried that Quattra would suddenly appear next to him again. He couldn't deny that the training had done him wonders, but damn if he wasn't a little traumatised by the lessons.

Watching him go, Quattra appeared pleased with herself. The young Adventurer had flourished under her tutelage; not only increasing his stats and ability levels, but also gaining new abilities from her. Plus, it was always nice to be afforded the opportunity to indulge in her two favourite hobbies: torturing people and breaking the newbies. Turning back inwards, she started yelling at some of the instructors who were allowing their students to lag behind.

A window popped up in Ishtar's vision.

Quest Completed! – Superior Training
You have finished the intense training by Captain Quattra.
Reward:
Stat increases
Ability Level Increases
New Abilities

He pulled up his status screen, curious to see if it had all really been worth it.

1H Weapon Proficiency Beginner Level 9
Heavy Armour Proficiency Beginner Level 9
Shield Proficiency Beginner Level 9
-

Skills:
Mining Beginner Level 1
Appraisal Beginner Level 5
Meditation Beginner Level 6

"Damn, now that's what I'm talking about!" Ishtar rejoiced. He made a mental reminder to go get revenge on those wolves at some point.

Ishtar was surprised that his passive abilities didn't appear on his status until he had actually used them, but looking at his status, he considered whether he should get some more magic strikes from the Mage Guild. Maybe even swing past the Adventurers Guild to see if there was a quest to take out the Night Wolves, since he planned on going to kill them anyway.

Checking his map, since he still hadn't explored that side of town much, Ishtar started walking —casually strolling around the areas that he hadn't yet seen, including the Castle at the centre of town. It was entirely covered in guards – oddly all Draconians. Then, he made his towards the Guild areas. Stopping at the Warrior Guild. At first, he found very little of interest, except for a small store with skill books. These were better options than waiting for training there. So, he got a new sword ability and a new shield ability for 2S each.

Ability Learnt:
Guard Beginner level 1
Increases Defence by 100% for 5 Seconds, can't move during that time

Ability Learnt:
Quick Thrust Beginner level 1
A thrust that attacks at double speed and increases user's movement by 200% for two seconds.

Heading to the Mage guild not far away, he once again went to the small store to buy some skill books. He got three starter abilities; surprised to see Mana Manipulation was a separate skill, as he didn't think his character needed it.

Ability Learnt:
Mana Manipulation Beginner level 1
Gives the user the ability to freely move and use their mana, including the ability to edit and create own spells

Ability Learnt:
Wind Strike Beginner level 1
A strike increased by the power of the wind.

Ability Learnt:
Stone Skin Beginner level 1
Increases natural defence by 200%, added to armour

He didn't bother with any fire-based abilities, due to his Race disadvantage. It wasn't worth it with the 50% extra cost. Maybe at a higher level, when he had mana to spare. There was one last thing he had to do in town, which was to go to the Adventurers Guild and check the Quest Board to see if there was anything on there about the Night Wolves. They were quite close to the town, considering it was still the starter town for Dracon.

Walking past the very few players that were still in their starter gear, Ishtar assumed a lot of players had moved to the other cities by now. He took note that school was in eight hours in real life, so he had a full in-game day before he had to sign out again.

Making it to the Adventurers Guild in short order, he looked over the Quest board. Besides all of the small-time gather-or-kill missions and some higher-level escort missions that would take days or weeks to complete, there was a note tucked in the corner of the board that contained precisely what he was hoping for.

F-Rank Quest Accepted! - Night Wolf Investigation

There has been an increasing number of attacks near River City by Night Wolves, previously never living this close to the city. The City Lord requests you investigate why they have moved closer to the City and if possible remove the threat from the city.

Gleeful to have found a quest for something he was already going to attempt, Ishtar was very nearly skipping as he left the Guild. A wicked smile appeared on his face as he walked down the street, causing citizens to shy away from him nervously. He didn't notice.

Getting back outside the city, Ishtar headed back to the area full of Horned Rabbits. This time, he saw a lot of Draconian killing them, and he assumed they were new players. On his way to the fringe of trees next to where he was killed by the Night Wolves, Ishtar found a solitary Horned Rabbit. He quickly killed and looted it to finish the Quest. He arrived at the trees and braced himself cautiously against the potential danger.

Shield up, and sword at the ready, Ishtar stepped between the trees before him and saw nothing. He assumed he needed to head further in to find anything, so he proceeded deeper. After walking for five or six minutes, Ishtar started to get confused. This group of trees didn't look like it should be this big from the outside.

Pulling out the map to study, he groaned in frustration. While the thatch of trees was narrow, tricking his initial perception into thinking that this

would be an easy task. They stretched on for miles
and miles, lengthwise – almost half a day's journey
from top to bottom. He was essentially searching for
a needle in a haystack.

After several more minutes of fruitless
searching, Ishtar began exploring outside of his path,
weaving left and right through the trees to cover
more ground. He had never been an outdoorsy kind
of person and had never learned any hunting skills in
real life. In the games he had played before, it was
always easy to find enemies – Ishtar wasn't aware of
just how many signs of animal activity and movement
he was missing.

Finally seeing a clearing to the side Ishtar
headed towards it, stopping just inside the trees and
looking around the clearing. Ishtar thanked his lucky
stars he had done so, as, near the other side of the
clearing there was a small hill with a cave entrance
slanting downwards. There were three Night Wolves
asleep near the entrance. Unsure if he could take all
three in a straight-up fight, Ishtar worked his way
around the clearing, staying shadowed in the trees
until he was almost to the side of the hill.

He got ready to try and rouse one of the
wolves, to pull it towards him. Ishtar found a stone
on the ground and threw it. His aim was terrible, and
he missed horribly, so he had to re-evaluate the idea.

Considering the increase in his stats, he decided to try and get a surprise attack in with the first one, before the other two could spring into action in time. As he moved forward, shield at the ready, he cast, "Stone skin," in a hush, activating his only defence spell.

As he got close enough to launch his attack on the first one, he stepped forward, swinging his sword towards the head in a brutal overhand strike while activating his favourite ability, "WATER STRIKE!"

CRITICAL STRIKE
Dealt 175 Damage
ONE HIT K/O

Beheading the wolf in a single strike was lucky, but unfortunately, alerted the other wolves to his presence at once. One leapt straight at him, quick as an arrow, while the other circled around him to flank him from his right.

Far more experienced now, after the last week of gruelling training and deadly sparring, Ishtar squared himself readily. His defence was excellent, so long as they didn't lunge straight for the vulnerable areas of his armour, like last time.

The first wolf lunged, teeth bared, and Ishtar timed his swing just right, dashing forwards and colliding with the wolf, activating, "SHIELD BASH."

Knowing that the wolf would be stunned for at least several seconds, Ishtar turned back to the second wolf coming up behind. He was just too late to defend against it, but the wolf only grazed his side, and the stone skin spell and his armour did their job well.

Moving back towards the first wolf, Ishtar quickly dropped his shield and because the basic broadsword had a larger than standard hilt used a 2H grip to increase the power of his attack.

"HEAVY STRIKE."

Two down, one to go, Ishtar thought triumphantly, though he knew this one was going to be the hardest without his shield. Having not trained much wielding a sword with both hands, Ishtar held it over his shoulder, hoping to get a fast and powerful rising strike as the wolf attacked him. Getting ready for his moment, the wolf had hesitated after he killed the second one, before appearing to become enraged. The Night Wolf's eyes started glowing red, and a shadow appeared over its front claws.

Worried that this ability could go seriously wrong, Ishtar got ready to use two of his newest abilities in conjunction, beginning to run at the wolf, quick, and low to the ground. The wolf lunged.

"QUICK THRUST; WIND STRIKE!"

Using the two abilities together, surprisingly, caused both his movement and thrust to increase in speed exponentially. Ishtar's broadsword speared the wolf right through the chest, shredding the flesh on its side and completely destroying its heart, along with half of its ribcage.

Not coming out entirely unscathed, Ishtar was hit by the wolf's Shadow Claw attack, launching him back several feet into the hard ground across the clearing. Ishtar lay on the ground, catching his breath for a few moments, before shoving the still bleeding carcass of the Night Wolf off and standing back up.

Received 70 Damage

You have successfully killed:
Night Wolf x3
You have gained 150exp.

Congratulations!
You have gained a level
You are now Level 3
+2 Str, +2 Int, +1 Vit, and 2 Free Stat points

After taking a few minutes to get his breath back and recover some more, he began looting the bodies receiving some meat and pelts. Once he got back to town, he would need to learn a cooking skill, and sell the pelts, since he'd forgotten before leaving town this time.

He found his shield near one of the headless wolf bodies, which promptly disappeared into dust, as he began to walk away towards the cave entrance. He was getting prepared, as he wasn't sure just how many wolves would be in there.

Walking through the cave, descending deeper underground, Ishtar began to notice that it was much smoother than he would have expected from a cave in the middle of some woods. He came to a split in the tunnel, giving him the choice of either left or right. Nothing distinguished either tunnel from the other, so he chose to go left, on a whim, and followed the cave as it spiralled further and further downwards. Ishtar finally started to hear something ahead, so he assumed he was nearing the bottom.

The cave opened into a vast hall that looked like the remnants of an ancient building, one large hall with multiple doors spread across the room. On the opposite side from where he entered, he saw another entrance.

"Seems it didn't matter which way I went", he thought. *"I guess I will leave that way just to make sure after I find the rest of these wolves."*

Walking into the hall, he found that the other end of the building had collapsed, as had all the doors bar one. Slowly moving towards that doorway, Ishtar was wary of attack. Going further down the hallway, the odd doorway appeared, but the rooms were empty of anything but bones and wolf shit. Finally, evidence of recent movement is seen: a dead wolf, half-eaten, against the wall. It reeked, which confused him. He decided to use appraisal on it.

Dead Night Wolf
This corpse is covered in small bite marks and other much larger ones. There is not enough evidence to say what caused the bite marks, but they were not made by other wolves.

The information worried him. He had no idea what he was stepping into. He reached the end of the hall, seeing more dead wolves that had been partially eaten. Stepping through the doorway, he could see a wall that had fallen, and broken a section of floor. Behind that section of wall and floor, there was a tunnel that looked like it was dug out by animals. What worried him, however, was that its circumference was probably an entire meter taller than he was. Looking further around the room, he could see the remains of the wolf cubs and several other big wolves. One was larger, and a different colour than the rest.

From where the wolves lay, he could see that whatever had come out of that tunnel had rushed in and killed all the cubs, some of the older wolves, and the alpha's mate. From what he gathered, the wolves were losing, and some ran away – likely the ones who were now attacking people near the city.

There was only one thing any good player could do: go deeper and investigate.

Chapter 7

Congratulations!
You have discovered a hidden Dungeon: Realm of the Rodent King.
He has been slumbering beneath the ground for many years.
His children come forth to devour all.
Step into his domain, if you dare!

You are the first player to have discovered a hidden dungeon.
+50 Fame
For this feat, you have been awarded +2 to all stats.

You have received the title:
"Seeker of the Hidden"
This title is cumulative for each secret place and hidden dungeon you find.
It adds +1 to all stats per level
You may only have one of your titles seen at a time. However, all benefits are retained.

Having all these screens appear as soon as he stepped foot at the start of the tunnel worried him a bit. The title, and what was written about the Dungeon, gave him an ominous feeling. Facing both the wolves, and what he assumed would be rats, had him hoping that his newfound skill would be enough for what he was about to face.

The cave was lit by a luminescent moss coating the walls. After a generous walk, it began to open up into a far more spacious area. Looking around, Ishtar saw three openings, as well as the dead bodies of two big rats – one a plain brown, and the other a smaller, sleeker black type. Deciding to try the left-hand path first, he followed the path once again.

As he walked, he heard a small scraping sound behind him. He gave a slight jump, and quickly spun around, looking for whatever had made the sound. Seeing nothing, he continued down the hall. Hearing the sound again he spun around, looking and searching. Once again, he found nothing.

Before Ishtar could so much as register his trepidation, he was suddenly hit from either side. One went low and the other high knocking him to the ground.

Received 20 Damage

Ishtar quickly jumped back to his feet, looking around wildly for whatever hit him. Hearing the scraping again, he lifted his shield in its direction and was immediately hit from behind at the same time a great impact hit his shield.

Received 10 Damage

Once again, he heard the scraping to his side. He assumed whatever was attacking him would follow the same pattern again, so he lifted his shield towards the sound. But, this time, he struck out in the other direction.

"QUICK THRUST!"

Dealt 25 Damage

Now that he had injured one, a health bar appeared. So he used his appraisal skill, trying to figure out just what his enemy was.

Shadow Rat
Type: *Beast* **Level:** *5*
This child of the Rodent King prefers to ambush its prey but is faster, yet weaker than most of its kind.

Now he saw through their strategy, as well as what they were; he was more than confident in his ability to kill them. Following the same pattern, he used to hurt the first one, it took only minutes to finish it off. Lastly, he listened for the final one, and activated, "SHIELD BASH" as it charged. Stunning, and knocking back the Rat, he then delivered a final blow, "HEAVY STRIKE."

You have successfully killed:
Shadow Rat x2
You have gained 200 Exp

Loot Menu:
2 Shadow Fur

Moving down the passage again, Ishtar was wary of more Shadow Rats appearing. After a short time, he began to notice a brighter glow, which he hoped meant a room. Getting closer, he saw a group of five rats – two of the Shadow Rats, two larger, brown rats that came up to his waist, and one even bigger, red rat. He again used Appraisal.

Burning Rat Lieutenant
Type: Beast **Level:** *7*
These fiery Rats can summon flames hot enough to melt iron. They control lesser rats in their position as a Lieutenant for the Rodent King.

Giant Rat
Type: Beast **Level:** *5*
These are just standard Rat grown to a massive size, they are the most ravenous of the lot, at times eating their victims while they still live.

Trusting in his newly increased stats, Ishtar ran straight into the left side of the room to attack the Giant Rat with a Shield Bash. It was stunned as he ran past, towards the Shadow Rat on that side of the room. Trying to dispatch the Shadow Rat quickly, Ishtar got ready to use a Heavy Strike. But, this time, when he thought of the trigger words he felt the system assist take charge, as his blade began to start its tell-tale glow. Swinging his blade, he solidly hit the rat in the head, flinging it back into the wall for increased damage.

Dealt 150 Damage

Dealt 45 Damage

When it didn't move again, he assumed he had killed it, and turned back to the Giant Rat.

Just as he was turning back around, he was hit by the Giant Rat, sending him flying. He bounced and rolled back to his feet, pressing back against the wall.

Received 35 Damage

Received 10 Damage

As it was charging at him again, Ishtar took a single step to the side and activated Guard just before the Giant Rat hit him. It impacted his shield at an angle and slammed into the wall, stunned yet again.

Dealt 10 Damage

Received 5 Damage

Jumping onto the Giant Rat, Ishtar used "Quick Thrust," three times in succession, straight into its head.

Dealt 50 Damage

Dealt 50 Damage

Dealt 50 Damage

Down to quarter health, one more decent hit, and the Giant Rat would die. Suddenly, it whipped its tail into Ishtar's head, rattling his skull, and disorienting him. It followed its attack by clamping its jaws down on Ishtar's side and slamming him into the ground.

Received 75 Damage
You are Bleeding!
You will lose 2 health every second for 20 seconds

Dropping his shield, Ishtar gripped his sword in both hands and stabbed towards the Giant Rat. Missing the first time, he kept stabbing in a frenzy. Not sure how many hit, and how many missed, he was just happy it eventually let go. He slumped to the ground next to its body.

Dealt 7 Damage

Dealt 7 Damage

Dealt 7 Damage

Dealt 7 Damage

Dealt 7 Damage

Dealt 7 Damage

Dealt 7 Damage

Dealt 7 Damage

You have successfully killed:
Giant Rat x1
Shadow Rat x1
You have received 175 Exp

Congratulations!
You have gained a level
You are now Level 4
+2 Str, +2 Int, +1 Vit and 2 Free Stat Points

Fortunately, the level up replenished his Health and Mana, so he could go straight through and use the same rough strategy on the remaining two rats. Quickly dispatching them netted Ishtar another 175 Exp. Ishtar saw the experience per level raised quite a bit with 2000 experience for his next level, he couldn't wait to get there and get stronger.

Now, it was time to face his true foe in this room. Since the creature was of the fire affinity, his plan included mainly using his Water Strike. As he advanced toward the Burning Rat, it finally took notice of him, and a wall of flame burst from its body as it charged. Ready, Ishtar raised his shield into position and activated Guard, yet the flames from the rat's fire still burned him.

Received 25 Damage.
You have been Burnt.
You will lose 2 health per second for 20 seconds
Movement reduced by 10%

He couldn't afford to take many more hits like that. Stepping back away from the Burning Rat, Ishtar tried to re-evaluate his enemy's abilities. It was bigger than the others, which compounded its threat, along with the flames licking from its body.

"Okay, new plan: no more running straight at it," he decided.

Advancing on the Burning Rat again, Ishtar waited for the Flame Wall ability to be used. When he got within a few meters of the Burning Rat, the fire again rose up. This time, instead of trying to defend against it Ishtar jumped and rolled to the side, coming up to the side of the Rat. Attacking with one of the sequences Quattra taught him, and using Water Strike with each blow, he managed to get in three solid hits, before the Burning Rat spun, and hit him with its tail, flinging him across the room.

Dealt 75 Damage

Dealt 75 Damage

Dealt 75 Damage

Received 73 Damage

Received 10 Damage

Seeing the Health Bar above the Burning Rat, he cursed as he saw that he had only removed about 25% of its health. Hoping it hadn't changed its pattern, Ishtar advanced again.

Sure enough, once he was close, the Burning Rat used the Flame Wall again. Ishtar dived out of the way, rolling to his feet, and moved in to do his water strike combo again. This time, instead of striking back at him, the Burning Rat began to shake, emanating thick steam. It then started to move a bit faster and, instead of a Flame Wall, it began rapidly shooting Fireballs at him.

Putting his shield in the guard position without activating the ability, Ishtar started backing away. Taking a small amount of splash damage for every Fireball that hit his shield, Ishtar ducked behind one of the Giant Rat carcasses and hunkered down.

Eventually, the fireballs stopped and Ishtar came out from behind what was left of the rat bodies. He strode quickly towards the Burning Rat, which was slumped over with exhaustion, and then used another Water Strike combo, taking a further 18% off the Burning Rats health.

Now, it was down to only 30%. Instead of steaming, it had burst into flames, and its speed had increased substantially. The Burning Rat charged straight at Ishtar, who tried to leap out of the way just a fraction too late, still getting hit with the Rat's flames.

Received 27 Damage
You have been Burnt
You will lose 2 health per second
Movement reduced by 10%

By the time he recovered, the Burning Rat was charging at him again. Only, this time, he decided to try something crazy.

He set himself ready for the attack beside the closest wall. Just as it was about to hit him, he took a quick step to the side, and used a Shield Bash, so that it hit the wall with full force. He was severely hurt by the Rat's flames in the process.

Received 73 Damage

Dealt 25 Damage

Dealt 10 Damage

Not being able to take a single more attack from the Burning Rat, Ishtar decided to try another combo. Using Heavy Strike and Water Strike together, Ishtar aimed at the Burning Rat's neck, severing its head.

Execution Strike

You have successfully killed:
Burning Rat Lieutenant x1
You have gained 250 Exp
You have gained an additional 50 Exp for the Execution Kill

Quest Received! – Burning Lock
You have defeated one of the two Burning Rat Lieutenants protecting treasure in this section of the tunnel system. Find and kill the other one for a greater prize.
Reward:
150 Exp, and the ability to open the hidden treasure chest.

Quest Received!! - Head-hunter
You have killed 2 enemies Execution style. Once you have killed 50, go to the temple of Vames to receive your prize.
Reward:
A title from the God of Death and Darkness

Quickly looting all the corpses for some more meat and pelts (he even got a Burning Rat pelt – Rare Grade), which would sell well if he could get it on the open market. He also found a necklace.

Pendant of Clotier
Type: *Jewellery* ***Durability:*** *45/50*
Quality: *Rare*
Clotier was a Mage, with a deathly fear of Rodents. His
Adventuring group forced him to enter these tunnels, looking for
the Rodent King.
+8 to Intelligence
+2 per second to Mana Recover

"Score! This is great for me. Keeping this one for myself. Really should find some companions, though. This is ridiculous, doing this by myself." Ishtar muttered.

Trekking back down the passage, towards the centre room, Ishtar equipped his new pendant and checked into why he could sub-vocally cast a spell. It seemed that it was a choice in settings that were already selected. It required more mana but was faster and better, especially if he was ever to fight another player.

After he got back to the centre room, he headed down the passageway on the right side and found a perfect replica of the room on the other side. The exact same methods that he used on the other side netted him another 600 Exp, and the loot of two Rat Meat, two Shadow Rat Pelt, Flaming Rat Pelt (Rare) and 2G.

Congratulations!
You have gained a level

100

You are now Level 5
+2 Str, +2 Int, +1 Vit and 2 Free Stat points

Quest Completed! - Burning Lock
You have killed the 2 Burning Rats guarding the treasure in this tunnel.
Reward:
150 Exp
The path to the treasure will now be open to you

Hearing a rumbling back down the passage had Ishtar running in that direction. Nothing new was in the tunnel, but once he returned to the centre room again, he saw a new opening in the ground.

Without his own source of light, and with no fire spells to speak of due to his Affinity, Ishtar looked around for something to light the hole. Ripping some of the moss off the walls, he threw it down into the hole. Fortunately for him, it only seemed to be about a metre deep, and the moss was still glowing strongly.

Jumping into the hole, Ishtar brushed aside the moss, revealing a long-forgotten tome. As soon as he saw the heavy volume, he could feel the power it exuded. He picked it up, and a prompt appeared.

Minor Heal
This light spell heals the target for 10× (user's intelligence level) up to a maximum of 500
Cost: *20 Mana*

Do you wish to learn this spell Yes/No

Stunned, since this spell would normally be impossible for any non-healer class to learn, Ishtar quickly hit yes.

"Now for the final tunnel. Shit, am I nervous to find this Rodent King. This really feels like I should have had a full team for this." Ishtar thought.

Making his way down the centre tunnel, Ishtar found a couple more caverns that were caved in, and many Rat carcasses of all kinds. Finally coming to what appeared to be an even bigger cave, Ishtar halted, shocked at what he saw.

Chapter 8: The Boss

Ishtar stepped into the biggest cavern he had seen yet. Looking around, he saw that there were three other openings in the wall, leading into other unseen areas of this underground labyrinth/ maze. In the middle of the Cavern, on a pile of bones, The Rodent King was being assaulted by a huge Night Wolf. Each cavern exit was guarded by two, only slightly smaller, Night Wolves. A few smaller ones were hugging the wall.

Ishtar saw that there was a great deal of Giant Rats and Shadow Rats trying to get in past the Night Wolves to help their King. He decided to use Appraisal on them all.

The Rodent King (UNIQUE)
Type: *Beast* **Level:** *13*
The King of his domain. His insatiable appetite for all things has his minions spreading out, killing and eating everything they can find, bringing tributes back to him.

Alpha Night Wolf (UNIQUE)
Type: *Beast* **Level:** *12*
The leader of his pack. His pack was destroyed, and their children were eaten by the Rodent King and his minions. He and his elite entered the Dungeon for revenge for his pack.

Elite Night Wolf
Type: *Beast* **Level:** *8*

Ishtar didn't know what to do. He was worried that they would all turn around and attack him if he stepped completely into the room. The Alpha Night Wolf appeared to be losing. He was down to less than half his original health, while the Rodent King still had about three-quarters remaining.

He decided to mentally toss a coin assuming that, no matter which side he helped, they would try to kill him afterwards. Ishtar used his new Heal spell on the Alpha wolf, while moving towards one of the doorways aiming to help the wolf there kill the rats trying to enter.

Looking back to the Alpha's health as he moved, he saw it increase by about 10%, racking up its health to over 4000. This was not a creature he stood a chance at killing alone if the beast decided to turn on Ishtar afterwards. His only chance was to help the Wolves, who were fewer in number, but also hope that they wouldn't successfully kill the King. He wanted to get the final hit, thereby claiming the rat's scalp as his own.

Arriving at the next entrance along the wall, Ishtar saw one of the two Wolves drop to the ground, dead. The rats could only attack the remaining wolves two at a time, the bodies of other rats obstructing the path before them.

Just as he arrived next to the wolf, it seemed to sense him, and turned Ishtar, baring its teeth, growling. He immediately jumped past the wolf and started hacking away at any Rat that got near him.

Not wanting to use most of his abilities, as they might hit the wolf, he only used Quick Thrust a few times at some of the Shadow Rats that got near. He also continued using Minor Heal on the Alpha behind him. He was trying to keep its health above 50%, but he was struggling to keep up with the damage the Rodent King was inflicting.

It didn't take long to kill the last five rats at this entrance. The wolf, now half-dead, went on ignoring him as it continued to guard the door. He couldn't afford the mana to heal it, so he just moved over to the next entrance, still guarded by two wolves. Just as he got to the opening, he spied a Shadow Rat slipping past them over the corpses of the already dead ones. Seeing it angling towards the smaller wolves in the corner, it barely made it five steps past them before Ishtar arrived near it, viciously using Shield Bash to slam it all the way back into a wall. Then, he followed it with a Quick Thrust to its heart.

For some reason, he was beginning to feel protective towards the smaller wolves near him, especially as they cowered from him, too injured to defend themselves. He threw another Minor Heal onto the Alpha. Checking The Rodent King, Ishtar saw that its health was getting closer to 50%.

Ishtar finally reached the last entrance, only one wolf was still alive, and it was dying fast, under the wrath of its final enemy – a Burning Rat. He used his combo move of Quick Thrust and Water Strike to inflict massive damage.

CRITICAL STRIKE
AFFINITY WEAKNESS
You have dealt 150 damage

The windows were starting to get in the way of his fighting. *"I'll have to see what I can do about that later,"* Ishtar thought to himself, as he dodged the returning swipe from the Burning Rat.

Just as he was about to strike again, the Elite Night Wolf to his side latched onto the throat of the Burning Rat and started whipping its head from side to side, reducing the Rat's health until it died seconds later.

With the entrance clear for the moment, Ishtar directed his attention back to the most important battle in the middle of the room, once again seeing that the Alpha Night Wolf was getting below 50% health. Ishtar used two Heals on the wolf to return its health.

The Rodent King was definitely winning the fight. It would have killed them all by now if he hadn't received his new Heal spell. In saying that, all four still-living Elite Night Wolves, having cleared their entrances, charged in at the Rodent King slashing at its sides, and doing substantial damage.

Within two minutes, one of the Elite Night Wolves had died, but they had gotten the Rodent King down to roughly 40%. Ishtar had been resting to try and refill his Mana, using a Minor Heal when the health of the Alpha dropped too low. This continued until the Rodent King reached 25% health. As soon as it happened, it bellowed and jumped back into the wall, collapsing two of the passages.

As it seemed stunned from hitting the walls, Ishtar quickly ran towards it, jumping, and activating Heavy Strike. He avoided using one of his Mana abilities, hoping to preserve it.

Dealt 22 damage

Shocked at how little damage he had done, Ishtar moved back from The Rodent King, just as the Alpha Night Wolf moved in to attack it again. Now confused as to why only the Alpha was attacking the King, Ishtar looked around just in time to see two of the Elites engulfed and killed by the number of Rat Minions that had come flooding through the one surviving entrance.

Ishtar moved to help the final Elite Night Wolf. Already, around ten Giant Rats, seven Shadow Rats, and one Burning Rat had been killed. Now, only two of the smaller ones, and one of the bigger rats remained.

Ishtar flanked the two shadow rats, using his Shield Bash on one while stabbing the other through the back of the head.

****CRITICAL STRIKE****
Dealt 59 damage.
You have Stunned the Shadow Rat

Looking up, as he started to swing at the Shadow Rat he'd stunned, he saw the Elite Night Wolf finish off the last Giant Rat. It turned, slashing out with its claws, and decapitated the Shadow Rat Ishtar had just stabbed.

"What a terrifying ability, glad the weaker ones never had that," Ishtar thought to himself, and quickly dispatched the stunned Shadow Rat with a Heavy Strike.

Having spent too long on this side of the room fighting, and getting distracted by the Elite Night Wolf, Ishtar checked back on the Alpha. Seeing that he was once again getting low on health, he used his Minor Heal as quickly as he could. Seriously worrying now, as he had less than a quarter of his mana left, Ishtar went back to the fight between the last Burning Rat and the Elite Night Wolf. Considering it was quite an equal fight, with them both sitting around half health, Ishtar went behind the Burning Rat and used his Water Strike on its tail, removing one of its most useful weapons. It reared back in pain, and the wolf capitalised on the lapse in attention, diving forwards, and crushing its throat, finally killing it.

Ishtar and the Elite Night Wolf stared at each other for just a moment, before they both moved back towards the fight between the Alpha Night Wolf and the Rodent King. The two Wolves used brilliant teamwork to reduce the Rodent King's health down to 15% within minutes. While Ishtar did very little damage, attempting to preserve what little Mana he had left.

Ishtar moved in to attack from the opposite side of the Elite Night Wolf, aiming to attack and separate the Rodent King's tail, just as he had done to the Burning Rat. Assuming the King would be sufficiently distracted, he didn't fear an attack. However, just as he was lifting his sword to strike, he was met by a powerful blow from the very part of the Rodent King he was about to assault.

Taking the brunt of that attack, the two wolves were able to sufficiently damage the Rodent King down to almost 12% health. One last swipe of the Alpha Night Wolf's claws and the Rodent King dropped even lower to 10%.

The King suddenly went berserk – hitting the Alpha Night Wolf backwards into the far wall next to

the cowering wolf, it then turned and bit the Elite
Night Wolf. It dove across the room, ramming into
the wall near the last opening, going deeper into the
tunnels.

As it hit the wall, the entire room rumbled.
Small rocks and dust began to shower down from the
roof as the tunnel collapsed. Large debris fell and hit
the Rodent King as well, reducing its health critically.

Ishtar, hoping it was stunned, rushed towards
it. Being the only two left in the fight, he assumed
that the Alpha would take charge. It was more of a
threat, and had already inflicted more damage than he
had. For that reason, Ishtar cast Minor Heal twice
more. Using the last bit of mana he could afford to
restore the wolf's health back to 20%.

Immediately, upon reaching the Rodent King,
Ishtar used what he hoped was the hardest hitting
combo yet – Quick Thrust, and then a pair of Heavy
Strikes. Each blow landed straight to the same point
on the creature's hind leg.

CRITICAL STRIKE
You have dealt 75 damage
*You have dealt a Crippling blow upon the Rodent King, and
have reduced its movement speed by 35%*

Ishtar was ecstatic that he was even capable
of inflicting damage on a boss of such a superior
level, much less anything above a minor injury. The

Rodent King started to turn towards him; he raised his shield and retreated slightly. By doing so, he created an opening for the Alpha Night Wolf to attack the King from the side. Ishtar wisely stepped back to watch.

It was amazing to watch, now that he had decided not to intervene. The Alpha Night Wolf moved with ferocious grace– almost fluid – while using just skills, and very few abilities. He had only seen the Alpha use two abilities. One had been a more powerful form of the Shadow Swipe used by the Elite, the other had caused its teeth to glow red as it bit down.

The Rodent King, on the other hand, had only used one. Besides the Minion Summon it had used before, it also used a tail swipe, of a silvery metallic colour. At the rate they were going, there was a good chance they would kill each other. Ishtar simply waited – eager at the idea of the loot ahead.

Watching the Rodent King drop to just a sliver of health, with the Alpha Night Wolf not far behind, Ishtar realised that he wanted the kill.

He began to move around, behind the Rodent King, just as it slapped the Alpha Night Wolf away. Ishtar jumped and tried flapping his wings to get that little bit higher so he could land on its back. Successfully landing near its tail, Ishtar ran along the Rodent King's back, towards its head, and activated

Wind Strike and Quick Thrust. He then stabbed straight down, into the back of the King. The sword sunk all the way to the hilt, and, just as he was worried he hadn't done enough damage, he felt a small amount of resistance. He believed this was its heart. The Rodent King squealed, and fell to its side, taking Ishtar along with it.

Ishtar looked down at the Rodent King, at its totally depleted health bar, and wondered why he hadn't gotten the notification that he had finished the fight.

Thinking to check on the Alpha Night Wolf, Ishtar moved over to where it was slumped onto the ground. The wolf that had been cowering in the corner had moved over next to it. Ishtar saw that the real reason it had been cowering was to protect a very small, snow-white wolf cub.

Not knowing whether or not to approach it, Ishtar just stood awkwardly near, until he heard a growling voice in his head. "Come closer Draconian. You may have the blood of my kin on your hands, but you have helped me defeat that which has killed almost my entire pack."

Ishtar cleared his throat, surprised. "Well, to be fair, I only killed the ones outside because some of them attacked me first. I wanted revenge, but I hate rats, so I decided I'd rather kill them instead," he said honestly. His words made the cowering wolf snarl at him, but the Alpha remained impassive.

"I understand. These are the rules of the forest: the strong must rule, and the weak must die. My mate is dead, and I am dying now. I would ask you take my last cub with you. She will not be welcomed by the remains of the pack."

The Alpha then growled at the smaller Night Wolf that had been protecting the cub. It shied away and quickly ran off with its tail between its legs.

"I will take her with me as a pet, then," Ishtar replied, trying not to show just how ecstatic he was at the idea. Free loot and a free companion – this quest really couldn't get any better at this point.

As soon as the wolf slumped over, dead, the windows he had been expecting appeared.

You have completed the Hidden Dungeon Realm of the Rodent King
As you are the first person to complete this Dungeon, you have been rewarded with the title:
"Bane of the Rodent"
Additional 10% damage to Rodents
Fame increased by 200

In Conjunction with the Night Wolf Pack, you have successfully killed:
23x Giant Rats

47x Shadow Rats
12x Burning Rats
1x The Rodent King
You have gained 75,000 Exp, as the only surviving participant of the fight.

Congratulations!
You have gained a Level x8
You are now level 13
+16 Str, +16 Int, +8 Vit and 16 Free Stat Points

You have received the Light Wolf pup as a Pet
Would you like to name her?
Yes/No

Ishtar sat, staring at the screen in shock at how much Exp he'd received.

Eager, but exhausted, he entered in the first name that came to mind: Snow. Unoriginal, maybe, but he wasn't in the mood to be creative after the task he'd somehow just managed to pull off. Striding back to the body of the Rodent King, he looted it.

Loot Menu
3x Shadow Fur
1x Burning Rat Pelt (Rare)
15G
Elemental Iron Sword
Take all Yes/No

Ishtar took the loot, intending to look at it all properly when he got back to town. Suddenly he heard a small voice in his head,

"Is my daddy dead?"

Turning back towards Snow, Ishtar saw her tentatively nuzzling the body of the Alpha Night Wolf with her nose. Ishtar, wanting to make her feel better, picked her up in his arms and cradled her. "I'm sorry, darlin'. He died saving you. He asked me to take care of you – said you were the most important thing in the world to him."

Hearing this, Snow climbed onto Ishtar's shoulder and snuggled into his clavicle. *"Thank you, Master. I will take care of you if you take care of me,"* she said sleepily.

On that note, Ishtar decided he was finished with this crazy Dungeon, and headed for the exit.

Chapter 9

Ishtar emerged from the cavern above the Dungeon, expecting to see the three Night Wolves respawned, only to find nothing there at all – just an empty clearing, surrounded by woods.

Figuring that the whole region had a very large time between respawns, he started the trip back to town. A seemingly quiet walk provided Ishtar with the opportunity to review his surroundings properly, as opposed to how he quickly scoured the area when looking for the cave. Looking upward, he saw a few neutral monsters that he was curious about, so he used Appraisal on the closest one.

Slavering Drop Bear (Neutral)
Type: *Beast* ***Level:*** *25*
This lazy animal sleeps for 16 hours a day but is very protective of its home. It eats anything it can reach and is known to drop from its tree onto Adventurers face at random, ripping them to pieces.

Seeing that the beast was way overleveled for him, Ishtar simply kept walking out of the woods. Exiting through the trees, Ishtar found the fields full of Horned Rabbits. As well as many more new players – more than last time.

Bewildered, Ishtar headed back into town, only to arrive at the Gate and be stopped by the guard.

"You need to pay the fee, Adventurer!"

"Fee? I've never paid a thing for entering this city," Ishtar protested, narrowing his eyes suspiciously.

"Not for you, for the beast. 50S to bring that thing into the city," responded the guard, eyes trained on where Snow's head was just starting to peek back up on the edge of his armour.

"Fine, but I'll be talking to your Captain about this when I see him," Ishtar promised, as he as he handed over the money.

At once, a piercing shriek sounded from absurdly close to Ishtar's ear.

"Oh my god! It's so cute! Can I pet it? Please?" a short, Catfolk girl in a pure white dress was reaching toward Snow, hands outstretched, as if about to pluck her from his grasp. Ishtar stepped lightly out of her reach and shook his head.

"Maybe some other time. I'm tired and logging off now. See you round," he waved amiably, walking away.

"I'll hold you to that!" the girl called behind him.

Upon getting back to the fountain, another window appeared.

SYSTEM-WIDE UPDATE IN 15 MINS.

NO MONSTERS WILL RESPAWN AGAIN. WE AT RUSTBEL HOPE YOU HAVE ENJOYED THE GAME SO FAR.

THIS UPDATE WILL REVOLUTIONISE THE REALISM OF THE GAMEPLAY. THIS WILL TAKE 24 HOURS.

We appreciate your compliance and purchase of Ariair Online

After reading the message, Ishtar logged off to sleep properly for the first time in over a week. He was looking forward to discussing this new update with his friends the next day.

*

Arriving at school the next morning, curiously without the aches and pains he had been waking up to the last few days, Jasper headed into homeroom to start the day. Arriving at the door, he saw that he was the first of his friends to arrive, so he took his habitual spot in the back corner of the room and looked around at his classmates.

Jono and Karl had been his only real friends since they met on their first day of high school, where they had all been reading the latest edition of a popular gaming magazine. Ever since, they had played the games together to a small extent, normally competing with each other to be the best, with each using a different class. They did this so that they could work together at higher levels when they wanted.

Spotting Jasper as he walked into the room, Jono hurried over to claim the seat next to him. "Hey, man. Feels like I haven't seen you in ages," he said.

Jasper chuckled. "We saw each other Friday, and it's Wednesday now. Really not that long," he pointed out, amused.

"Yeah, but, with the time difference, it's more like a week and a half," Jono pointed out happily.

"Try closer to two weeks but I know what you mean, it's easy to lose track," Jasper answered with a chuckle.

With how excited and loud Jono was being, the rest of the class had begun to give him weird looks. Except a few who seemed to be wryly amused, used to his loud personality. A few were even nodding in agreement, clearly having played the game as well.

Just as the bell rang, Karl slipped into the room and sat down seconds before their teacher walked in, giving the other two boys a quick nod in greeting.

As homeroom finally concluded, the boys exited back out into the hallway to make their way to their first class.

"Talk to you guys at lunch – I wanna know about your progress so far, and what the hell is up with this update," Karl said, before waving goodbye and walking ahead of them before they could get a chance to greet him properly.

Jasper and Jono exchanged a look before heading to their own classes.

*

Jasper walked into the cafeteria to find Jono and Karl already at their usual table.

Taking his seat without a word, Jasper purposefully ignored Jono as he leisurely made extra-sure that his lunch tray was parallel to the table, drawing it out, just to be an ass, until Jono looked like he was about to explode.

Jasper couldn't help but crack a smile before relenting with a short huff of laughter. "So, how are you guys doing in the game so far? And what do you think this update will be about? Like, the game has only been out four days in Real Life."

As per usual, Jono jumped straight in as soon as Jasper finished talking. "Dude, this game is freaking amazing! I'm already level twenty! I'm playing as a Vampire Nightblade, which is just… so freaking cool. I mean, I get penalised during the day, but at night-time, and in caves, I get way stronger," he enthused animatedly.

Karl raised a curious eyebrow. "Nightblade, huh? What happened to your usual choice of ranged characters? Usually, I'm the one with the DPS types – how are we gonna play together if we both are? Since I'm a Sun Elf assassin," he added importantly.

"I wanted to fuck shit up," Jono answered simply, with a grin. "Besides, isn't that a stupid combo? It's legitimately in the name – sun assassin," he shook his head with a chuckle. "Sounds like fun though. We can be a pure attack group, I guess, or just find someone else to heal."

"It'll be fine," Jasper said. "I'm a Draconian Elemental Knight, and I found a healing spell in a Secret Dungeon, so I can play a healer as well. As long as you guys buy me mana potions. Though, if that doesn't work, I did meet a cute healer yesterday. She's a Catfolk."

Both Jono and Karl just stared at Jasper in shock; their jaws pretty much hitting the table.

"The hell, dude? Just how?" Karl exclaimed.

"Lucky dick," Jono said, an impressed grin on his face nonetheless.

Jasper laughed sheepishly. "I got lucky," he admitted. "I'm only a level thirteen – I just have decent stats because I trained with this crazy-strong instructor down at the guards' training grounds. Oh, and I kind of won custody of this baby wolf cub. I named her 'Snow' because she's a mutated Night Wolf."

"Wait, what?" Jono said, confused. "I thought you could only get training at the guild you got your job at? Like how that's the only place you can go to upgrade your abilities once they reach level nine."

"I did my first quest for a Guard Captain, and then gained some rapport with the rest of the guards. I guess that had something to do with it," Jasper supposed with a shrug. "Anyway, forget about it. What's with the update? Increasing the realism?"

"Never mind that, what about that cute healer girl you mentioned?" Karl grinned lasciviously.

Unbeknownst to the boys, a girl at the table next to them perked up at the mention of the pet wolf. Turning to eavesdrop, she focused on their conversation, before her attention was called back by her annoyed friend.

"Jess? Jessica! Are you listening to me?"

Jessica smiled sheepishly. "Sorry, got distracted – just remembering a promise I made yesterday," she responded.

*

After school, Jasper made his way to Yamoto Dojo; the dojo where he had been beaten up by that douche a few days before.

"Good to see Glen is original," Jasper chuckled as he walked in the door.

Without the haze of utter disorientation to mar Jasper's perception of the place, he took the chance to look around properly, curious. There were three separate rooms on the main floor, interconnecting to a spacious main room, with softer flooring, and a mirrored wall. He peered through one of the doors to see another room that looked pretty much identical, only much smaller. The final room was storage space, full of racking, containing wooden swords, and shields in various shapes and sizes. Some shelves had clothes on them, and a secured area with a security door was at the rear of the room.

He walked up to the door of the office and knocked. Upon hearing a "come in," Jasper opened the door and stepped inside.

"Hi, Glen," greeted Jasper.

"Jasper, come in. How are you feeling? What have you been up to? You look better. Are you here to sign up for the beginner class we are starting tonight?" Glen responded.

"I'm feeling much better than the last time I was here. I've been playing this new full-immersion VRMMORPG called Ariair Online. Honestly, I didn't know what your class schedule was like, so I came by to check it out. But, if there is a class, I can join tonight?" Jasper asked enthusiastically.

"Honestly, I have no idea what a V...M...R... thing is, but it's good to hear nonetheless. Considering how we met, this might be good for you. Though I should mention, you won't really learn how to wield a sword or fight that quickly. You need to focus on strength and flexibility first and foremost," Glen said, switching to a more serious tone.

"It stands for Virtual Reality Mass-Multiplayer Online Role-Playing Game. Sounds good, though. I'm looking forward to learning from you," Jasper said.

Since he had to wait anyway, Glen asked Jasper to help him set up for the class.

*

A half-hour later, the room was set up. They had placed a rack of wooden swords, various body weights, and some soft foam blocks around the room.

By the time Jasper had changed into the clothes he had been given (called a Gi, by Glen), another fourteen people had arrived and were milling around the room.

Jasper stood off to the side, waiting, until he noticed the rest of the class approach the mat, bowing their heads, and kneeling in ranks. Jasper followed suit. Their Sensei soon joined them on the mat.

"Welcome to your first class, everyone. This beginner class will be taking place twice a week from 4pm. If you haven't met me yet, my name is Glen Yamoto, and I am the master of this dojo. My father was Japanese, so I was raised on martial arts and learning to fight in general. I expect you all to call me Sensei during class.

"This is a purely beginner class, so we will be going through general exercises to strengthen your bodies, while also touching on parts of martial arts, and the different forms of sword fighting we teach here. In this beginner class, we will start with a form of two-handed German Longsword. After you advance to a more advanced class, you can choose which path you wish to follow, or continue doing both martial arts and sword training. Do we have any questions?"

In response to Glen's speech, a smattering of, "No, Sensei," came from around the room; around half not saying anything at all.

"Good. Now, to begin with, we will start with some strength work," said Glen, with what Jasper would later swear was a malicious grin.

What came next was one of the hardest hours of Jasper's life. For the first half hour, they were doing supersets of exercises – alternating between core work, sprints, and push-ups. Then, while hurting already, Glen started teaching the class a couple beginner guards, going through The Ox, The Plow, The Fool, The Roof, and The Tail. These were the basic stances and guards from ancient times. Glen went through them all, fixing their footwork, as well as body and arm positioning, during the process.

This made it even harder to get everything right, with how sore Jasper already was. He thought he did alright, considering his foot placement was only fixed slightly, and he mixed up which guard was which a few times.

By the time the class finished, Jasper was bone-weary but delighted that he had chosen to start this experience. As about half the class remained, bombarding Glen with questions, Jasper just waved on his way out of the door and headed home to resume playing Ariair Online some more. His mind preoccupied with this big new update.

*

Glen was impressed with his new class, but especially Jasper. He had met the boy just days before but, somehow, he already seemed slimmer, and fitter.

After the last members of the new class had left, Glen went to his computer and looked up the game. After half an hour of looking into the headset for Ariair Online, Glen was utterly intrigued.

According to a study that had been investigating the Rustbel VR headset, the headset wasn't perfect. Instead of completely putting the body into a form of sleep paralysis, it just lulls the body to a state of almost lucid dreaming where every movement the user made in the game caused the body to tense and make micromovements, which reacted like exercising.

Chapter 10 – Mana Manipulation

Welcome to our game-changing update. We know you were just getting used to the control, but we decided you were getting it too easy. Think of the game as hard mode now. Enjoy yourself now, we know we will.

Yours sincerely,
The Gods, who are now officially in charge.

Pain level can now be changed between 20% up to 100%, there will be some benefits to changing it to 100%

Mana Manipulation is a must for all magic users.

Mana conductivity of metals is now taken into account.

That's all we are telling you about. Figure out the rest for yourself.

Ishtar stood dumbfounded at the message that appeared when he logged back on. Going through his settings, Ishtar decided to change the pain level up to 100% just to see what the benefits were, assuming he can always change it back later. While he was fiddling with them, he stopped any damage notifications from appearing while in battle, now the only thing that would appear was the health bar of his enemy.

"Hmmm, so this is what that message meant by game-changing…I think I'm a little screwed with this bronze armour and going to have to rely on my non-magic attacks more. Also, I need to figure out how to use magic again." Ishtar muttered to himself.

Looking down at his armoured chest, Ishtar checked on Snow. He assumed she disappeared the same as he did while he was logged off, she was still sleeping soundly with a cute little snore/growl every now and then.

Ishtar sat down on the side of the fountain and started meditating in an attempt to sense where his mana came from. Directing the slight magic sense he gained with Mana Manipulation towards his own body, Ishtar couldn't figure out where his mana came from at first, but he started trying to sense the mana flow in his body. After half an hour of quiet meditation and finding nothing, Ishtar stopped, frustrated. He looked around the area, and in the distance, he spied the looming citadel of the Mage's tower. Figuring that was a point of interest to visit, Ishtar set off in the direction of the spire.

He hadn't spent much time in the Mages tower before, having stopped there just long enough to buy some spells from their store. Upon entering through the gates to the tower's inner sanctum, Ishtar walked past many annoyed-looking players standing in line outside the store near the door to the tower.

Ishtar walked into the tower and approached the receptionist.

Before he could even open his mouth, the receptionist spoke "Another one wanting to learn Mana Manipulation? Go back outside with the rest of the others and buy the skill book. Then you can come back and I can actually help you."

"Actually, I already have the skill and just need the help with it. I can't seem to access my mana," Jasper replied.

The receptionist seemed surprised that he had the Mana Manipulation ability, chuckling when he got to the end of his sentence. She picked up a small silver bracelet from her desk, paused for a moment then spoke into it. "Can I get a teaching apprentice to come into the atrium" she then looked back at Ishtar and said, "That will cost you 20S for the lesson you are about to have please,"

Just as Ishtar had removed the 20S from his inventory and handed it to the receptionist a figure shrouded in a long black cloak with the hood up walked up to him and said in a feminine voice, "Please follow me to a teaching room,"

She immediately turned and started walking deeper into the building. Ishtar quickly followed, looking around and surveying his surroundings. Down the hall were various paintings on the walls and with the odd niche holding a vase or statue of a wizardly figure. They had walked down many various hallways before Ishtar noticed that on many of the walls there were some runes, barely perceptible, but definitely there.

Unsure of how to fill the silence, Ishtar spoke, "We have been walking for some time, but the outside building didn't seem quite this big,"

The figure turned back to him and replied with a hint of scorn in a higher pitched feminine voice, "Of course the building is bigger on the inside, did you really believe that this small tower could hold everything needed for one of the largest branches of the Mages Guild in Dracon? The whole building has been covered by runes made by Spatial and Void Mages. There are also defence runes spread throughout the building, it's basically indestructible," by the end the figure sounded smug, "We are almost there, this next door is our room,"

Ishtar followed the hooded woman through the door, the room was a small square room with a bookshelf in one corner and a table against the wall next to it. His instructor crossed the room to sit on a set of pillows. Ishtar followed her, she turned to him and removed her hood as she sat. She was a pretty Catfolk with a calico pattern across her ears and hair, but he couldn't see more than that due to her cloak.

"Take off your armour and sit down Ishtar," she said in an annoyed tone, "my name is Jahani, and I'm an apprentice Lightning Mage that is being made to teach you today,"

Ishtar removed his armour, he was only in a linen top and pants and placed a still sleeping Snow next to him and sat down before replying "What do you mean Lightning? I thought you could only specialise in one of the six base affinities?"

"Clearly, you're an idiot then. That's stupid! I have an almost equal affinity for Fire and Air, so I'm suited to magic from both the school of Fire and Air and their combination Lightning." Jahani snapped.

"Oh yeah, I get it now. Can you tell me more about the combinations please?" Ishtar said as he was starting to regret getting saddled with this particular Catgirl as a teacher.

"Only three more weeks before I can leave, only three more weeks," Jahani muttered to herself before answering Ishtar, "Well I have to, don't I? Part of my apprenticeship consists of teaching young and/or new students," said Jahani.

Switching to a more serious voice, she continued,

"So due to there being only four primary elements that can be mixed together as Light and

Dark are opposites and can't normally be mixed with the primary four. The combinations are Magma, the mix of Earth and Fire; Lightning, the mix of Fire and Air; Ice, the mix of Air and Water; and finally Mud, the mix of Water and Earth."

Jahani paused for a drink of water she pulled from her inventory before leaving it next to her. Ishtar assumed this meant she would be doing a lot more talking.

"These affinities won't appear on your status page until you learn a spell from their respective field and then their percentage will be the average between their "parent" primary affinities. You understand?" Jahani continued.

"Uhh, kinda...though I have spells from both Earth and Air yet under my Affinity tab on my status page all it said was Water with no further detail?" Ishtar asked.

In her snide tone, she retorted, "Well clearly you're an idiot", in her more serious, "teacher" voice Jahani continued "Your status page will only show basic information until you actually learn more about the particular information then it will be updated on your status page."

Status
Name: *Ishtar*
Alignment: *Neutral*

Level: *13*   **Exp:** *10910/18000*
Class: *Elemental Knight*
Race: *Water Draconian*
Money: *16G 95S 50C* **Gender:** *Male*
Title: *Seeker of the Hidden*
Fame: *260*   **Infamy:** *0*

-

Health: *310/310*   **Health Regen:** *2.6/Sec*
Mana: *560/560*   **Mana Regen:** *15.5/Sec*
Stamina: *300/300*   **Stamina Regen:** *5.0 /Sec*

-

Strength: *48 (59)*   **Dexterity:** *24 (25)*
Agility: *22 (23)*   **Endurance:** *29 (30)*
Vitality: *31 (32)*   **Intelligence:** *48 (61)*
Wisdom: *23 (24)*   **Luck:** *12 (13)*
Free Stat Points: *24*

-

Affinity:
Water: 100
Air: 30
Earth: 30
Light: 30

After checking his status page and seeing the newer design without skills or abilities, Ishtar noticed his affinity list had actually been updated.

"So, my status says Water is at one hundred and Earth, Air and Light are each at thirty. I'm assuming Fire, Dark and none of the combination elements is on there because I don't have any spells from those schools?" asked Ishtar.

"Exactly. You're actually picking this up faster than I expected," Jahani answered with the first genuine smile directed towards Ishtar.

"The hell? She actually is really good at teaching, then why was she such a bitch before?" Ishtar thought to himself as she continued in her "teacher" voice.

"I am impressed a Water Affinity Draconian like you, judging on your colouring, has an equal affinity in two opposing elements like Air and Earth. Normally one would be stronger than the other," Jahani stated in a slightly confused tone.

"Well before this lesson from you the only affinity information I had was just that my base Affinity was Water. The increase is from using those spells I think." Ishtar said.

"Well you must have some affinity with all the Elements besides Fire, your base opposite, then as spells would have barely worked. Unless of course, you had an item that gave or increased your affinities?" said Jahani.

Ishtar sheepishly removed the Iron Elemental Sword from his gear and handed it to Jahani and said: "You mean like this sword I recently got from a dungeon?"

Iron Elemental Broadsword
Type: Broadsword Durability: 100/100
Quality: Uncommon Damage:15-25
+30 to all Affinities
+10 Str
+5 Int
A well-made iron blade made specifically for an Elemental Knight

After inspecting the sword Jahani looked to Ishtar, exclaiming, "Yes! Exactly like this sword you dolt! That sword accounts for most of your affinity points in everything except Water. Forget about it now. I need to get on with the actual purpose of this lesson and teach you to access and use your Mana Well. Hopefully, this doesn't take long so I can get back to more important things." she continued after a moment "To begin, start lightly meditating, I trust you can actually do that properly?"

"Yeah yeah I can do that," Ishtar replied. She gestured for him to seat himself and tentatively gave him encouragement to start a trance.

Jahani's voice took on a droning hypnotic quality as she started talking again, "Feel the mana in the atmosphere around you. Since your primary element is Water, think of the Mana as the spray at the bottom of a waterfall. It's floating, spreading away and around you, surrounding you in it's a cool touch. Picture, it, feel it, what does it look like? What does it feel like? What does it taste like? Expand your senses."

Skill Learnt:
Mana Sense Beginner level 1
You can now see the mana around you.

Unbeknownst to Ishtar as he opened his eyes they had started to glow a brilliant neon blue as he answered Jahani's questions. "I see it, it's like a morning fog rolling off the ocean that is everywhere all the time, but I can somehow see through it. Except when it gets near you, and it starts getting darker and slightly changing colour."

"Good, now direct your senses inside you. You're looking for the point where the Mana connects to your body. There should be a point where it looks like it is being sucked in." Jahani continued.

Using his new Mana Sense Ishtar watched how the mana swirled around his body. As he was Meditating Ishtar saw that at the centre of his chest the mana appeared to become a whirlpool as it was sucked into his body. He was so shocked by this, he accidentally stopped meditating and turned to Jahani,

"It feels like there is a whirlpool right here in the centre of my chest, but it stopped just after I noticed it. I can still feel something there though".

"That whirlpool feeling was the increased regeneration of your mana made possible by your meditation ability. I asked you to use it because the increased rate makes it easier to see. You lost the feeling because you stopped meditating. Start again, and this time direct your senses into that spot, it's where your mana well is. Tell me what it looks like. It normally looks different for each person." Jahani replied.

Following her directions Ishtar started meditating again, he directed his senses to follow the mana whirlpool into his chest until he found what he was looking for,

.

"In my mind's eye or whatever you want to call it, it appears to be a silver lake. Although hanging above it is six points of light. One for each of the main six elements. The blue light representing Water is beautiful, it undulates between the crystal-clear blue of a lake to the dark blue of a stormy ocean. None of the others do that, and it's also much brighter than the others. I can barely see the red of Fire though it's still there. Together they make a six-point star." Ishtar describes.

"That makes sense, they are your affinities, apparently heavily affected just by having that sword though it seems they would have appeared either way with you. I don't understand how but you seem almost to be a true Elementalist, though it means you will never get some of the benefits people who specialise get. You shouldn't be able to get an affinity with Fire though due to your body being of the Water affinity. You also have to have a small affinity with pure mana since your lake is Silver." Jahani stated.

With curiosity, Ishtar asked, "If everyone's mana well looks different to them, what does yours look like?"

"My mana pool looks like a massive storm front to me. Full of dark red and green clouds, with flashes of yellow like lightning. As I run out of mana, the clouds disappear. Therefore, I believed I was perfect to specialise in Lightning magic. It is generally considered that mana pools are unique to each individual, it takes the form of the person's primary elements as well as being influenced by their general thoughts." Jahani explained.

"Wow, your mana pool sounds rather beautiful. A dangerous storm for a dangerous Mage." Ishtar complimented Jahani. She was rather cute and he hoped she would be less rude if she was in a better mood.

In response to his compliment, Jahani blushed and continued with her lesson.

"Well...now that you have sensed your mana well it's time to try and use it. Go back into your inner mana well, with your senses feel around your "lake", feel the sides, pick a spot you like and form yourself a dam gate. Once you have made it, open it slightly and let a little mana out before closing your gate back up. Use your will to control that mana as it enters your body, move it through your body, down your arm and release it out of your hand towards the empty part of that wall to your right." continued Jahani.

Following the instructions, Ishtar felt his mana move up through his chest and back down his arm where he aimed at the wall off to his left that was blank. Just as the mana reached his hand, a silver bolt shot out and slashed against the wall. A large silver rune, taking up a large part of the wall, began to glow.

Ability Learnt:
Mana Bolt Beginner level 1
A simple mid-range attack spell with no element

What neither Ishtar nor Jahani were expecting was a blinding flash of white light radiating out from Snow, as she had also been following the lesson Jahani had been giving Ishtar.

Your Pet Snow has accessed her Magic for the first time.
She has gained Light Affinity
She has learnt Flash
She has learnt Light Globe
She has learnt Light Claw
+200 Exp
Snow has gained a level

Snow is now Level 2

"Snow you are simply amazing, you grasped magic quicker than me," Ishtar exclaimed to his pet who he had thought was still sleeping.

"I wanted to be more helpful to you Master, you have taken me in when my father died, and the rest of my pack rejected me. I just want to be stronger," Snow replied.

"Well done, you even managed to make the defence rune activate. I didn't expect such a simple spell to have enough power to activate it. Your pet is also fascinating, where did you get her?" Jahani asked.

"I found a hidden dungeon where her Father, an Alpha Night Wolf was killed by a Rodent King. I helped his pack kill it, and since she was a genetic throwback as a Light Wolf the pack wasn't going to accept her. The Alpha told her to become my pet with one of his dying breaths," Ishtar answered.

"But now you can use your mana manipulation, so our lesson has come to an end. Now you can leave, and I can get back to training. Farewell Ishtar, you were faster and more intelligent than I expected. Maybe I will see you again when I become an Adventurer as I am almost finished my apprenticeship and hope to become one when I do so. Good luck for your future."

"And to you Jahani, and to you" Ishtar answered as he picked up his gear and replaced it, Snow following him as he left.

Chapter 11

As Ishtar left the training room, he was still in a state of shock at how quickly Snow unlocked her magic. He would have to help level her up in the hope she would be helpful for him in a real fight. He assumed it was innate to her race of Light Wolf after watching the Night Wolves fight, but he still expected to have to raise her level up a few times before she was capable of using it.

Entering the entrance hall of the Tower Ishtar noticed it was now full of those players who were previously lined up at the shop several hours before when he first entered the Tower. They were slowly being led away one by one by different apprentices entirely covered by their black robes with their cowl raised.

Seeing how all these players had moved into the entrance hall, Ishtar hoped it meant the shop was now mostly empty and that he could actually get in there to find out how to upgrade his spells since some of them have been stuck at the peak of Beginner Level nine.

The shop still had two other customers when Ishtar entered, so he decided to have a look around while the shop worker finished helping the other customers. The stock was heavily geared towards pure mages, as up to a third of the store was dedicated to just robes in varying cuts and styles, which he assumed gave different buffs depending on the colour. A quarter of what remained had different displays of wands and staves, with just a few weapons or armours that would be suitable for him when he was a much higher level with a much fatter purse.

Ishtar made his way to the display of rings and pendants that he was currently lacking. Most were also well out of his level and price range, with even the mid-tier stock increasing health by a percentage or increasing mental stats by up to twenty-five. They were also priced in the hundreds of gold. Ishtar spent some time looking at the low-quality stock and decided to buy two rings, one that increased his health by 50 and one that reduced his armour penalty towards mana by 10% for 5G each.

Ishtar also looked at the pendants, but his Pendant of Clotier was far better than anything he could currently afford. Seeing the other two people exit the store Ishtar walked over to the counter with his chosen rings.

Before he could speak himself, the nearby shopkeeper interjected, "Are you another one of the travellers that need the mana manipulation ability book?" He spoke with a slight greedy grin.

"No thanks, I already had the ability before the Gods threw us into the deep end by changing how our abilities work in the world" Ishtar responded. "I'm actually here to find out how to upgrade some of my combat spells that have stalled at the peak of Beginner Level nine, oh and I also want these two rings" Ishtar continued.

The shopkeeper seemed to deflate slightly as his greedy grin disappeared, "Oh, a regular customer. Well if you are going from Beginner to Basic in your sword spells it will cost 25S per upgrade. Be warned they do change name when you upgrade if you use a vocal cast,"

Ability Upgraded:
Water Blade Beginner Level 9 >> Blades of Water Basic Level 1
Create a second blade made from the water surrounding your actual blade that doubles the width of your sword and increases the length by 1m.

"You can also learn Ice Dagger and Lightning Shock as you have reached Level 10. They will be 1G each. Other than that, come back when you have gotten other spells to the peak of Beginner Level nine." the shopkeeper finished.

"Fantastic. I will take all of that, please. Thanks for all your help" Ishtar answered putting as much gratitude into his voice as he could, knowing that it can be very important to be on this NPC's good side in the hope he could get a discount in future.

"Your total will be 12G and 25S."

Ishtar handed the shopkeeper 12G and 50S, "The extra is for the information. I'll come back to see you when I can upgrade my abilities or afford some more of your fantastic stock," Ishtar said, finishing the conversation.

Ishtar waved to the shopkeeper as he left. Just as he was exiting the shop, he saw that a name appeared above the shopkeeper's head in green writing. Considering the name of low importance, he vowed to check it next time he visited. Just outside the door, Ishtar opened both of the ability books to gain them, knowing he couldn't use the Lightning spell due to the need for the Fire Affinity. With the sword, he could fix that issue counteracting the deficits of his race.

Ability Learnt:
Ice Dagger Beginner level 1
A 5-inch dagger made of Ice that materialises in the casters
Off-Hand that will melt after one minute
Cost: 100 Mana

Ability Learnt:
Lightning Shock Beginner level 1
An electric current is injected into the user's weapon that will
explode out on contact with the next struck object
Cost: 50 Mana

Pleased with his new items and spells Ishtar made his way to the Warriors Guild to upgrade his other abilities that had reached the peak of Beginner Level nine.

Arriving at the training ground for the Warriors Guild Ishtar couldn't tell the difference between the players and the NPC's as they were running drills together.

"The AI running the personality for these NPC's is truly amazing, I can't fault the believability and force behind their personalities as they interact with us players." Ishtar mused to himself.

Moving towards a Draconian standing off to the side watching over the men and women training, Ishtar stopped a few feet away before speaking.

"Excuse me sir, my name is Ishtar, and I need to upgrade some of my Proficiencies and abilities," Ishtar said, introducing himself.

"Welcome to my training ground Ishtar, I am Captain Cromias. The abilities are easy enough to upgrade, you just visit the tent behind me, pay the standard fee, and you will receive the upgrade. The proficiencies, on the other hand, are a lot more difficult for you. You need to prove to a trainer that you have increased your skill with your weapons and armour before your increase is granted." The Draconian replied.

Looking past the draconian Ishtar saw the tent he had been referred to.

"Ok then. I will go upgrade my ability and then come back to you for the test to upgrade my 1H Proficiency, Shield Proficiency and Heavy Armour Proficiency." Ishtar replied.

"Sounds good lad." the Captain replied.

With that conversation finished Ishtar moved past the Captain and entered the tent. This time it only took him moments to pay for the upgrade to his ability as he didn't get an explanation.

Ishtar thanked the shopkeeper as he left on his way back to Captain Cromias.

"Ok Captain, I'm ready to try this challenge," Ishtar declared with a grin, he was starting to enjoy fighting.

"I should mention that it costs 1G per attempt to take the upgrade challenge. If you don't perform well enough, you will have to try again. You don't have to win, just prove that you have improved your fighting abilities enough to be considered of Basic ability instead of still a Beginner." Captain Cromias answered.

The Captain suddenly turned away from Ishtar and yelled out to one of his subordinates, an instructor.

"Proctor I need a challenger for a Beginner one-handed and Shield proficiency challenge!"

The instructor thought for a moment before calling out to the group he was supervising,

"Rando, you are Basic Level one in two-handed Sword, and Medium armour are you not?"

"Yes, Proctor Sir", came the answer,

"Well get over to Captain Cromias then," Proctor answered.

Proctor turned back to the Captain, "One of my best young talents sir."

Rando was a 6'2" hulking Catkin more reminiscent of a Lion, though had a shorter mane than many of the other Catkin Ishtar had seen. He was clad in a matching set of black leather armour, with some familiar looking fur on the collar. As he moved closer, Ishtar saw the armour better and decided it was very likely the armour was made from Night Wolves. Strapped to Rando's back was a nasty-looking iron Claymore. Ishtar quietly hoped Rando didn't fight as well as some others he had seen, or else he would lose badly. Given Rando's immense physique, Ishtar's doubt grew and grew.

Wanting to get a better feeling for his new enemy Ishtar used Appraisal on Rando.

Status
Name: *Rando*   **Level:** *10*
Class: *Berserker* **Race:** *Catkin (Lion)*
Health: *310/310*   **Health Regen:** *18.6/Sec*
Mana: *70/70*   **Mana Regen:** *2.5/Sec*
Stamina: *420/420*   **Stamina Regen:** *23.0/Sec*
-

Strength: *46*   **Dexterity:** *32*
Agility: *38*   **Endurance:** *42*
Vitality: *31*   **Intelligence:** *7*
Wisdom: *5*   **Luck:** *16*

Even though Rando was two levels below Ishtar, his physical stats were fairly similar since he was actually a Berserker with no magic, unlike Ishtar. Ishtar would have to thank that sadist Quattra one of these days since he had similar physical stats to Warriors. Though since Rando had better abilities than him, Ishtar decided to use some of the free stat points he had been saving up. He added 7 to Strength for more powerful strikes, 4 to Agility to increase his movement speed, 10 to Vitality to increase health to 470 and finally 6 to Endurance to increase his Stamina. He only hoped the additions he applied gave him the added chance to win.

While still looking at his Status Page Ishtar was interrupted in his thoughts by Captain Cromias,

"Oh, and before I forget, Ishtar, you're not allowed to use any of your spells in this fight and Rando won't use any of his Berserker abilities; you can only use the standard Warrior abilities that you would know."

Ishtar looked down at Snow, who had been following at her usual place just next to his left knee for a moment before speaking, "Go wait over by the Captain for me sweetheart."

"Yes, master. Good luck. You can take him" she responded before moving to lie down just behind Captain Cromias.

A square the size of a tennis court was cleared in front of Captain Cromias with Ishtar and Rando in the middle. They both looked at each other for a long moment before bowing slightly. Ishtar was a bit nervous since he was about to have his first fight with the pain levels at 100%.

Ishtar withdrew his sword from its scabbard and equipped his shield before taking a guarded stance. Across from him, Rando removed his Claymore from his back, put the sword on his right shoulder, took a half step forward and bent his knees before leaning forwards slightly.

They both stayed as still as they could, just waiting for the signal to start. With a piercing yell, Captain Cromias signalled the start, "BEGIN!"

Almost instantly Rando glowed a blood red and surged forward, sweeping his sword wide as he attacked Ishtar. Ishtar barely got his shield up in time to block the strike. The strike was so powerful that his arm went numb for a moment, and he was knocked back two steps.

Slightly off-balance Ishtar had no choice but to step back to regain his balance, his shield up protecting his left side in case Rando struck him again. Looking back to where he was a moment ago Ishtar saw that Rando was just standing there with a smirk on his face. Deciding to take the initiative, Ishtar charged forward to his assailant. As he was a half-step away from the still unmoving Rando, he used Shield Bash, only just clipping him. He followed it up with a Quick Thrust, but that was mostly deflected by Rando, the blade barely nicking his right hip.

With that nick, Rando's health bar appeared above his head and Ishtar saw he did barely any damage at all.

Rando once again started moving towards Ishtar, only his sword now glowing red. Worried, Ishtar used his Guard ability this time. Rando struck at Ishtar's shield with crushing force, again and again, each strike coming harder and faster. Ishtar heard a crack come from his shield. Ten strikes were involved in the flurry that Ishtar assumed was the Berserker class ability Frenzy Strike. Ishtar expected the fight to be called off there, though after waiting a few seconds no call had been made.

Once again Rando paused as soon as he finished his strikes. Ishtar took this advantage to attack, trying out his new Cleave ability. Ishtar's sword glowed white and accelerated as he swung his sword in a downward slash. Just as the sword got near Rando, he started moving again and managed to get his claymore up to guard against Ishtar's strike. Ishtar's sword managed to cut through the armour on Rando's chest before his sword was deflected away. Rando was knocked back by the Cleave, the hit taking almost a quarter damage. Ishtar knew he wasn't going to be able to use that ability again, due to its cool-down. Finally doing some real damage to Rando but with a numb shield arm, Ishtar grinned, he was starting to enjoy this.

Rando pulled out a small flask and took a large drink. Ishtar sniffed a strong smell of alcohol before the stopper was put back on the flask.

"Wooo, let's take this up a notch. **Blood Rage**," Rando said with a chuckle.

Red-Black steam started releasing from Rando's body, eventually clouding him. Suddenly a shattering impact was inflicted on Ishtar's shield, finally breaking it off his arm to fall to the ground. Barely able to move his arm but ignoring the incredible pain he was in, Ishtar frantically looked around for Rando. There was a blur to his left, but when he turned towards it, he was hit in the back with a blunt impact that felt like the back of Rando's sword. It would appear that Rando had decided to just play with him. The impact had caused a crack in Ishtar's chestplate.

Ishtar was at less than half health now, and each strike from Rando had started doing more damage. He was constantly trying to catch up with the rapidly moving Rando who was slowly losing health due to his ability. He had been able to block a few of Rando's blows but not many due to the speed his opponent was moving. Ishtar started to realise that Rando was moving in a pattern, constantly striking his left, doing a full circuit around him before striking his back then starting all over again. Ishtar tried to fight smarter since he knew he couldn't keep up with the rapidly moving Catfolk, relying on his educated guess. Just as Rando was about to strike his left again, Ishtar aimed a Quick Thrust at the spot he anticipated Rando to be. He barely managed to hit his enemy. Waiting for the next opportunity he tried again as he was about to be struck in the back. This time, his aim was perfect, and he pierced Rando directly through his chest.

"STOP, the fight is over," Captain Cromias screamed suddenly.

Ishtar removed his sword from Rando's chest and stepped back only to see just then that Rando only had a sliver of health left. One of the members of the audience ran up to Rando and forced a potion down his throat. Once his health started moving back upwards, the healer came over and gave one to Ishtar as well.

Five minutes later they were both exhausted sitting on the ground next to each other with full health again but still with very little stamina. Ishtar had won somehow against the cheating Berserker Catkin, but both his shield and Breastplate had been broken. In the meantime, all the observers had returned back to their groups, Ishtar spying a fair bit of money changing hands. Apparently, not many people had bet he would win even with his armour and level advantage. Captain Cromias walked over to the two fighters sitting on the ground and said, "Congratulations Ishtar, you have shown your growth in fighting by combating on par with an enemy that had higher ability level than you. I am happy to agree that you have passed this challenge."

Quest Completed! – Prove Yourself
You have proven your skill with the blade in a fight for your life.
Reward:
Upgrade to your Proficiencies

Ability Upgraded:
1H Weapon Proficiency Beginner Level 9 >> 1H Weapon Proficiency Basic Level 1
10% additional damage with 1H Weapons
Greater understanding of fighting with 1H Weapons
3% increase to Swing Speed

Ability Upgraded:
Shield Proficiency Beginner Level 9 >> Shield Proficiency Basic Level 1
Blocks additional 15% impact and damage.

Ability Upgraded:
Heavy Armour Proficiency Beginner Level 9 >> Heavy Armour Proficiency Basic Level 1
Movement Penalty reduced by 5%
Reduces impact of strikes against the user by 5%

Ishtar said his goodbyes as he got up and left with a snoring Snow in his arm. Now that his broken equipment had been stored in his inventory, it was time to hand in his very first quest.

*

Walking back to the gate that Captain Kieras had his office, Ishtar noticed there were not as many confused-looking players as earlier. He guessed he was far behind the ball on that one, with the in-game week he spent with the slave driver Quattra.

Ishtar luckily found that Captain Kieras was already at the gate when he arrived.

"Captain, I have completed the quest you asked me. Here are the Rabbit Horns I collected from the ones I have killed." Ishtar said

"Lad, good to see you. You sure seem stronger than last time I saw you. Clearly, you have had some interesting times." Kieras replied.

Quest Completed! – Thinning the Herd
You have become the bane of the bunny population
Reward:
75 Exp
25C

"Well I imagine you have other business to attend to, so good luck Ishtar." finished Kieras.

157

Once again Ishtar was on his way with just a wave as he left, his next stop was to the Adventurers Guild to hand in his Night Wolf quest.

*

Ishtar entered the Adventurer's Guild, spying the counter where he would conclude the quest he had been assigned. He patiently waited for the last person to leave before stepping up to the counter itself.

"Hi, I would like to turn in the Night Wolf Investigation Quest. The Wolf Pack has left the area, and the only reason they were attacking was that they were being attacked through a broken wall in their den." Ishtar immediately told the Receptionist.

The female Draconian behind the counter looks confused for a moment before a look of recognition appeared on her face.

"Ah sir, we will need to verify your information. Can you please give the location to me and we will have an investigation team out there within the hour?" she requested.

Ishtar quickly gave her the map coordinates for the entrance in the woods before wandering to the Tavern on the other side of the room. It was full of roughly-dressed but well-armed men and women sitting at tables. He sat down to eat some food and have a drink while he waited.

An hour and a half and some very average food and weak beer later Ishtar found himself sitting near the counter on the official side of the building. A nondescript being in dark clothing with their hood up in a way that no detail was seen of who was under it appeared next to the counter. Ishtar blinked, and before he could comprehend the flurry of movement, the figure disappeared. As soon as the figure had departed the receptionist, she quickly walked out of the room and up a set of stairs that had been hidden behind a door.

Five minutes later the receptionist came back down the stairs and approached Ishtar, "Sir, the Guildmaster would like to talk to you about what was found at the coordinates you gave us. Please follow me," she instructed him.

Ishtar nodded and followed behind her as they mounted the stairs. At the top of the stairs there wasn't a hallway - as Ishtar expected to find - but just another door that the receptionist knocked upon. There was a muffled confirmation, and she opened the door and ushered Ishtar inside, closing the door behind him.

Ishtar looked around the small office, on his left was a wall of windows with a door in the middle that looked onto a balcony and over a garden. On the right wall were the heads of beasts he had never seen or imagined before. Opposite him was a desk flanked by two bookcases, some of the books glowed to his eyes, which he assumed contained a high level of magic. Finally, behind the desk was, much to Ishtar's surprise, a Drow.

Ishtar's immediate response was to splutter, "But how?! Your race doesn't belong here!"

"Hahahahaha I never get tired of that response. Not many people get to come into this office Ishtar, especially green recruits like you. Though not many Adventurers, in general, manage what you have recently." The Guildmaster responded.

"What do you mean?" Ishtar asked.

"Well since we aren't acquainted before now. My name is Jevan Nion'leas and I am the Guildmaster here, I was sent here for pissing off some of my superiors on the Lost Continent. In case you didn't know all the Guilds are worldwide. But the reason you are here is because someone of your level could never have defeated an Elite Night Wolf let alone the Alpha and a Rodent King. And before you ask, our investigation team does have the ability to determine what was killed in the area for quite some time after it happened even after the Gods have removed the body." said the Guildmaster with a sardonic grin.

Ishtar proceeded to explain what happened between his first death to the Night Wolf, to the finding of the hidden dungeon and also teaming up with the Wolves, all the way up to him claiming Snow as to her father's dying will.

His story even surprised Guildmaster Jevan, "Well, looks like you had a hard time and came out the other side much stronger with a loyal companion. You have even solved our problem with the Night Wolves, now that most the pack is dead and the remaining ones have left. Due to the enhanced difficulty of the quest and the fact you completed it alone, I'm going to award you with an increase to Rank E along with other rewards."

Quest Completed!!! - Night Wolf Investigation
You have not only found out why the Night Wolves were attacking people near town and had the pack leave the area but helped destroy an even deadlier enemy that was going to be coming next.
Reward:
Upgrade to Rank E
15,000 Exp
15G

Congratulations!
You have gained a level
You are now Level 14
+2 Str, +2 Int, +1 Vit and 2 Free Stat points

Chapter 12 – Back into Dungeon Diving

Surprised by how his meeting with the Guildmaster had transpired, Ishtar left the office in a slight daze. His first action was to walk back to the receptionist and hand her his Brown card, he was handed back a Red one. He next walked over to the Quest Board to see if there were any appropriate E or F quests for him. Scanning the board, he found a collection quest in the forest west of town, an escort quest that went to the to a small village halfway between River City and Cindera to the north, and dead centre of the E Rank quests he found what he needed to finish multiple quests.

Quest Accepted!
Clear the Abandoned Mine
E Rank Group Quest
The Lord of River City requests a group of Adventurers to clear out a Den of Spiders that have taken up residence in an Iron Mine in the Miditarac Hills. This is needed for future expansions of River City. It is advised to have a party of at least 3 members as the number of Spiders are unknown.
Reward:
5G
5000 Exp
1 Skill Book
Additional Rewards for any unique treasures

Ishtar was slightly worried about the last line of the quest information, like there was something he wasn't being told or that he was being played. Figuring with him as a Tank/Healer and Snow as a DPS with her Magic they could finish the quest by themselves, as long as she got some levels before they got there. Taking the quest information to the counter, he retrieved his upgraded Red E rank card and accepted the quest.

On his way out, he bought an identical replacement of his Shield and Chestplate from the small store in the Guildhall for 50C since it was second-hand repaired beginner armour.

*

Opening his map as he was exiting the gate, Ishtar saw the marker on his map that he assumed indicated the entrance to the Mines. Just outside of town he saw another standard MMO starter enemy, Boars. Ishtar quickly used Appraisal on the nearest one.

Boar
Type: *Beast* **Level:** *2*
A simple beast that is useful only for its meat

He continued analysing many other of the hogs, as many seemed to be larger than others from an initial glance. As he looked further and further from the city, Ishtar noticed the levels of the boars rise, slowly becoming more of a challenge the further away from the city he searched.

Ishtar told Snow to use her Flash ability to blind the closest Boar before moving forward to use Light Claw. This combo blinded the Boar stunning it for a second and took off around a quarter of its health before Ishtar immediately stabbed it in the head, killing it instantly. Unfortunately, Snow didn't get any experience from this and Ishtar only got 1 Exp himself. Ishtar had Snow use the same initial combo on the next closest Boar, but this time instead of killing it, Ishtar used Shield Bash to knock it to the ground stunning it for five seconds. Snow then used her Light Claw again before biting down and ripping out the Boar's throat killing it. This time Snow got the full 10 Exp from the level two Boar. It would appear with Pets that they only got Exp when they made the kill themselves, or maybe when they participated in a combat quest, they might share the quest experience. He would have to find out later.

With a grin, Ishtar moved towards the next target, a level three Boar.

*

By the time Ishtar and Snow had arrived at the start of the hills that lead to the mine, Snow had reached level five and had grown a few inches taller and longer. Soon she wouldn't fit in his arms while sleeping anymore. He checked her stats.

Status
Name: *Snow*
Race: *Light Wolf*
Level: *5*
Experience: *400/2000*
Health: *150/150*   **Health Regen:** *0.4/Sec*
Mana: *180/180*   **Mana Regen:** *7.0/Sec*
Stamina: *140/140*   **Stamina Regen:** *15.0/Sec*

-

Strength: *20*   **Dexterity:** *12*
Agility: *23*   **Endurance:** *14*
Vitality: *15*   **Intelligence:** *18*
Wisdom: *12*   **Luck:** *10*
Free Stat Points: *8*

-

So, it seemed her stats were skewed towards the physical because she was a wolf, with a bit extra added towards Intelligence and Wisdom because of her added Light affinity/Magic. He also wondered whether training could increase her stats like they could his. Nevertheless, he decided to quickly get to the Mine to start the quest and kill some Spiders. Ishtar knew that he would also have to put actual work into training Snow up for a while during this quest, without taking all the kills himself.

Ishtar would have to wait till he watched Snow fight some more to see where he wanted to add the free stat points that Snow had. Whether she needed to be quicker, have more mana or be stronger would depend on how they fought together as she grew. As the free stat points increased, she could quickly increase one stat or multiple if need be.

*

Arriving near the mine entrance, Ishtar saw that there was a small town nearby with what appeared to be a small smelter and processing facility. Apparently, this town had decided to do all the work and make the ingots here rather than send out raw ore. Moving through the seemingly nameless town, Ishtar noticed many of the buildings were dilapidated and broken. Clearly, it had been abandoned for quite some time. For such a desolate location, Ishtar wondered just why the quest had even been created. He smelt a rat. There was much more going on than he was being told, even if it was just that the city needed more resources to implement some plan.

Ishtar looked down at Snow and said, "I guess it's time for us to hunt some spiders, I will need you to use your Light Globe though as I didn't get any torches before we left town."

Ishtar and Snow walk through the entrance, with the light filtered in from outside Ishtar could see little more than a few metres ahead. Worried about what was beyond that distance, Ishtar had Snow cast the Light Globe before they actually entered.

You have entered the Black Blood Lair
*The Black Blood Spider Queen has taken up residence in the
formerly-known Miditarac Iron Mine and started breeding*

So as not to blind themselves Ishtar had
Snow make the glowing globe hover above and
behind them. The start of the mine is built well and
reinforced with thick wooden beams, oddly enough
no webs or any signs of spiders were seen at the
entrance.

Slowly advancing down the passage, Ishtar
could hear nothing except Snow and himself
breathing and the crunch of the odd stone beneath
their feet. The light from Snow's Light Globe only
showed a roughly seven-metre circle around them. It
wasn't until they had walked around fifty metres
down the passage that it started to open up into what
appeared to be a small natural cavern that had a small
amount of web around the sides. Ishtar still saw very
little evidence of the spiders he was supposed to be
hunting, though he now had the option of four
different paths in front of him. Being unable to
decide, he picked up a small stone off the ground
threw it in the air straight up and waited to see which
direction it bounced once it hit the ground.

The stone bounced to the left of him.
Following the rock's instruction, he walked down the
new section of the tunnel, eventually seeing an
opening into the next room. Snow's Light Globe

wasn't bright enough to show much of the room, however.

"Snow can you make your Globe rise up over the room, so we can see more of it?" Ishtar asked her.

Instead of responding to him Snow's spell slowly floated past Ishtar and into the room. By the time it moved into the room properly, Ishtar could see the first enemy, a 1m tall Spider so dark it appeared to be blending into the shadows even when the ball of light was shining onto it. He used Appraisal,

Black Blood Spider
***Type:** Arachnid **Level:** 10*
This breed of spider prefers dark places, they have evolved in a unique way that even their blood is now black, so it can't be seen in the dark. Their eyes are very sensitive to light

The Globe finally got high enough to show the whole room dimly, and it turned out there were three of the spiders, all level 10. Fortunately for Snow and Ishtar, they were spread throughout the large room, so they could attack them individually without drawing the others.

Slowly moving towards the first one, Ishtar told Snow his plan to kill the arachnid.

"Snow, when I get close to the first one, I need you to use your Flash spell to blind it, so I can attack it while it can't see me." he directed.

As soon as he finished talking to Snow, he advanced towards the closest one.

"Now Snow!" he yelled as he closed his eyes as hard as he could, even through his eyelids he could see the brilliant flash of her spell. Upon opening his eyes he saw the Spider with its legs curled up underneath it and its red eyes sightless. Using Cleave on the right side of the Spider, his upgraded ability had the sword glow a blood red increasing the sharpness and speed of his downward swing, cutting completely through all four legs on that side of its body. The spider fell onto its side, bleeding out and keening. Its health at once dropped below half with his critical strike and was quickly dropping more since it was bleeding out from the stumps of its former legs.

"Snow use Light Claw on its eyes to keep it blinded," Ishtar ordered.

Snow leapt forwards, her right claws shone briefly as she swiped at the face of the Spider, taking a further 20% of its health. With roughly 25% left and all but paralysed Ishtar wanted Snow to get the experience from the kill as she was half its level. Ishtar moved to the spiders right, so he wouldn't get hit by what remained of its limbs and rapidly stabbed it in the side twice taking off a further 10% of its health.

"Snow finish it" Ishtar stated as he looked around to where the other two spiders were. By the time he had turned back, Snow had killed the spider. Ishtar decided to quickly loot the carcass before using the same strategy on the other two spiders. It only took a further ten minutes to finish off the other two spiders and collect their loot. The loot was nothing special, only three Pieces of Black Blood Spider Carapace.

You have successfully killed:
Black Blood Spiders x3
Your Pet Snow inflicted the final blow
She has gained 1050 Exp

Pausing for long enough to refill both his own mana and Snow's, Ishtar decided to continue following the left-hand wall. This led him into a small alcove that looked empty even with the Light Globe.

SPIT

In reflex Ishtar raised his shield in the direction of the sound, an impact hit his shield almost straight away. A slight sizzling came from the impact point on his shield, looking down at it Ishtar saw that was starting to melt. He dropped his shield into the dirt hoping it would stop melting before destroying the equipment, as Snow moved closer to him her

Globe finally revealed the back of the alcove. It was full of webbing. Halfway up the wall was a different kind of spider, it looked similar to the standard Black Blood Spiders but with a green stripe running down its back.

It started to shy away from Snow's Light Globe, so Ishtar tried using the same strategy he had used with the other spiders. Snow used Flash, the Spider fell off the wall, but when Ishtar moved forwards to attack it started spitting its poison again, this time blindly.

SPIT *SPIT*

Ishtar leapt to his left out of the way and watched the spots on the ground where the poison hit. It sizzled for three seconds before disappearing into smoke, which was good news for his shield. The Spider was stunned once it hit the ground and Ishtar and Snow managed to kill it quickly between them, this time Ishtar didn't leave the kill for Snow. He just kept stabbing and slashing until it died.

You have successfully killed:
Black Blood Poisonspitter x1
Your Pet Snow inflicted the final blow
She has gained 350 Exp

Fortunately, Snow appeared to have attained the last strike before the spider's death and was rewarded for her luck. She had just reached level six, and he hoped that he could get her up to level ten before they left the Mine.

Picking up his shield, Ishtar noticed it was slightly melted, pausing for a moment to check it before he continued to follow the wall around to the left. Ishtar found another tunnel and entered it with Snow at his side. As he went further into the dimness, the cut of the stone got cleaner, the walls and floors even looked polished. Not far past the polished areas, Ishtar found a door. Being an intrepid adventurer, naturally, he tried to open it…

…and it was locked. Not being a rogue with lockpicking ability or a Mage with some spell to do the job, Ishtar decided to use the other skill in his repertoire; the brute force approach. He started kicking the lock on the door. It took five kicks before the door started to splinter around the lock, three more kicks finally broke through the door. Beyond the opening, he found a small office that he assumed belonged to the Foreman. Just a small desk with the remains of a couple chairs to the side, with a bigger more expensive looking desk on the other side. Nothing else was in the office other than a small cupboard in the corner. Whoever cleared out the office when the Spiders moved into the mine did a wonderful job of taking everything that wasn't too big to easily carry.

Ishtar relaxed and sat down. Remembering the last fight, Ishtar realised in the slight panic of the poison being spat at him he had completely forgotten to use any of his abilities. He was now annoyed at himself. He thought to himself that with some of the fights he had been in he shouldn't be so jumpy just because it was dark and... He was scared of the dark... a little bit.

"Stupid Spiders, this game is just too real," Ishtar muttered.

Being an experienced gamer, Ishtar started to rummage through the area with more focus. The drawers in the desk were empty as per expected. Ishtar quickly looked inside the cupboard and also found that empty, taking a step back he saw a glint of metal wedged between the cupboard and the wall. He leaned in and grabbed the object to find out it was a Steel Pickaxe, he used Appraisal on the object.

Foreman's Steel Pickaxe
Type: Axe **Durability:** *150/150*
Quality: Rare **Damage:** *15-25*
+10 to Mining
+15 Str
Increase Mining Speed by 45%
Unable to be used in combat
A very rare Pickaxe that was specifically made for Foreman Aniga of the Miditarac Iron Mine

It was pretty damn good. Especially since the one he was given by Coal was just a Bronze Pickaxe. Also, the faster he could mine ore the faster he could finish this semi-dungeon and get back to finish the quest.

Putting the Pickaxe in his bag he left the office and once again followed the left wall around, he ended up back in where he thought he had begun. The next tunnel around was his next aim, he walked down it and found a small room with a deposit of ore. Ishtar moved over to a deposit on his left, it was the size of his chest, so he took his brand-new pickaxe and started working at it. It took him five minutes for him to get the first decent size piece of ore out of the wall, twenty-five minutes later he had finally depleted the whole deposit. He got a total of fifteen pieces of ore in the end.

Seeing that he was finished with this room, Ishtar retracted his steps once again and moved to the next tunnel. Slowly moving down the tunnel, Ishtar wondered what he would find in this next room.

Arriving at the entrance to the next open room, Ishtar kept Snow just behind him with her Light Globe above them. Snow moved the globe into the room and as it illuminated the first row of spiders, half the size of the first Black Blood Spiders they had fought, the spiders began to scuttle towards them. Just as they got close enough for Ishtar to try and use Appraisal, Snow's Light Globe disappeared…

"SNOW RUN AWAY, I CAN'T SEE ANY OF THEM," Ishtar yelled.

Ishtar and Snow quickly turned around and started running with the sounds of skittering legs fast catching up with them.

"Snow use Light Globe again," Ishtar ordered.

The Globe appeared behind him as he ran ahead of Snow, he risked a quick look back only to see Snow get caught in the webbing on the side of the tunnel and be swarmed by the horde of smaller Spiders. Ishtar turned around to help her, just as he turned he watched her health hit zero. Incredibly upset as he didn't know if he could summon her back, Ishtar started running again until he got back to the room he thought was the entrance room and continued to follow the wall to the left.

Ishtar had forgotten there was another tunnel in that direction.

He ran down that tunnel hoping he had lost all the Spiders that decided to follow him. He frequently stumbled without any light and ran face first into the end of the tunnel, losing 25HP in the process.

Ishtar shook his head and took a step to the right in an attempt to steady himself on the wall. But, instead of his hand making contact with the wall that should have been there, Ishtar just fell sideways and started to slide downwards.

Chapter 13

"Oww, eat a bag of dicks gravity," exclaimed Ishtar, referencing a popular character from a TV show.

"Love that show. Still hurt like a son of a bitch." Ishtar continued to talk to himself to alleviate some tension.

He opened his eyes again after falling down what he assumed was a hidden set of stairs. Ishtar noticed some new notifications that he ignored, wanting to see more of the area around him first. Considering the amount of pain he was in, Ishtar was a little worried to check his health to see how close he came to dying, after falling down those stairs. Slowly flicking his eyes to the top left of his HUD, he saw his Health was only about 10%. Even his Stamina was almost non-existent, to fix this he used his Heal spell a few times while resting, this got his Health back up to 75% and his Stamina to 30% in short order.

Once he knew he would survive Ishtar quickly checked on the status of Snow, he was relieved to find a small picture of her face with a timer on it. He had been worried that he wouldn't be able to revive her.

Standing up, Ishtar looked around to see where he had ended up after his tumble. The area was surprisingly lit well enough that he could see the whole area around him. Turning around to look at the way he entered the area he saw that he wasn't going to be able to leave the same way, as the opening to the stairs was around two metres off the ground. Ishtar saw that he was surrounded by massive boulders, as though this area was either a natural cavern or had caved in at some point in time. He was also surprised that there was actually light. He looked up to the room and saw many clear crystal formations that were scattered over what portion of the ceiling he could see. Ishtar couldn't see past the first lot of boulders, so he didn't know if there were any enemies in the room or not.

Knowing the only way was forward, Ishtar threaded his way through the surrounding rocks. As he rounded the boulders, what he found on the other side shocked him greatly. The cavern was quite large and barren, except for on the other side of the open cavern where there was an oddly familiar temple. He couldn't place it, but he also couldn't shake the feeling of familiarity.

Slowly moving across towards the temple, Ishtar was wary of being attacked, yet he was surprised he still hadn't seen a single monster. Still moving slowly but starting to pick up speed as his Stamina regenerated, Ishtar skirted a large boulder that had fallen and crushed part of the stairs.

As he got closer to the temple itself, his eyes drinking in as much detail as he could, Ishtar saw many broken statues, which appeared to have been intentionally destroyed. The base that the statue had stood upon was untouched, but the largest piece of any statue that he could see was half of a hooded face. Looking up at the temple itself, Ishtar assumed the game's designers were influenced by Ancient Greek architecture since the columns were reminiscent of the pictures he had seen of the Acropolis.

Though other than the broken statues there was very little damage to be seen. Most of the visible damage could be very well attributed to the temple being under the mine, with the rocks falling from the roof and just general age wear. How the temple got underground when it looked like it should be in a city square, Ishtar couldn't figure out. He was sure he would need to figure out who the temple was dedicated to, so he could investigate the lore behind it being here.

Going through the entrance door Ishtar expected to see depictions or symbols denoting to whom the temple was a tribute, but once again the targeted damage was enacted with broken statues and defaced walls.

He entered the beautiful hall that was simply decorated in shades of a deep blue with a smattering of gold, likely the colours of the dirt and dust that had settled into place over the years the temple had been underground. There were stone pews on the opposite side of the room with a narrow path on either side of them, and another larger destroyed statue at the front of the pews. The path seemed to go behind the statue with a half wall behind the pedestal used as a backdrop for the statue that was there. On the left side from where he had entered was a large and ornate set of doors and on the opposite side was a much smaller single door.

Assuming the nicer things would be behind the ornate doors, Ishtar walked towards and through them. On the other side, he found a hallway full of doors. He tried the first door and found a meeting room with a long table featured in its centre. The next room was bigger with tiered benches, which Ishtar assumed was a teaching room. All of the rooms down the corridor turned out to be meeting rooms, teaching rooms and a few were set up for crafting. All in all, the exploration was a complete bust for Ishtar.

Trekking back to the first hall, Ishtar walked over to the other side where the first room was a long dormitory, probably for the young novices. There was also a series of other single or double rooms, for either higher level Priests or Visitors, and a sickbay that had been cleared out of any loot. There was only one more room at the end of the hall before Ishtar considered this side bereft of spoils. Entering the room, Ishtar could tell from just the quality of the decor that this room was for whoever was in charge of the Temple, such as the High Priest or Priestess.

The room was actually separated into two: a seating area with comfortable looking chairs and a desk in the corner still covered in paperwork, and a bedroom. Checking the bedroom first came up with nothing of value, everything that could have been worth money was either too big and heavy or deteriorated from age. Investigating the desk next found Ishtar rummaging through the desk drawers. The paperwork he discovered fell apart in his hands as he tried to pick it up to read, and it wasn't until he got to the bottom drawer before he finally found something of interest.

Ishtar was removing his hand from the drawer when a small part of the desk caught on his hand. It moved slightly back to where it started, curious, Ishtar pushed the piece properly. Once it wouldn't move any further, it clicked into place, and a small panel of the side of the desk clunked open. Inside the small opening was a small soft bag, opening the drawstring on the bag Ishtar found a small pyramid-shaped jewel, it was a smoky black gem with the "smokiness" appearing to move inside the jewel. Ishtar used appraisal on the Jewel but just got a screen covered in question marks. Clearly, his skill wasn't good enough to get the real information of this rock.

After placing the jewel back into the bag and the bag into his inventory, Ishtar exited the room. He walked out the door that was just next to the room and found what would have once been a beautiful garden. It took up a similar amount of space as the first hall he had entered through, with a veranda around the outside. Ishtar could only dream what it would have looked like when this place was still in use.

A small pond nestled in the middle of the yard, flanked by small stone benches all across the area. It would have been a tranquil place to meditate or just spend an afternoon studying for the novices, maybe even would have had a good view of the stars when on the surface. Since there was a doorway here and another that he didn't go through on the meeting/crafting/learning side and as he assumed this is where the path behind the pseudo wall was going to lead, Ishtar wondered if there was also a doorway to his right at the back of the garden.

Reaching the back of the garden courtyard, Ishtar saw a break in the wall that looked as though it would have been a secret passage at one time. Sitting next to the break was a boulder that must have broken from the roof of the veranda and hit the wall. Ishtar squeezed through the opening, only to find another door. Opening the door, Ishtar found a set of spiralling stairs heading further into the ground.

Hoping to find some real treasure Ishtar started his way down the stairs. Fifteen minutes later Ishtar finally hit the bottom of the stairs and found a small chamber with a set of midnight black doors that had silver depictions of different races bowing before a robed figure. There was a silver pedestal in the middle of the room and looking up, Ishtar saw the roof was also black with the light in the room, similar to the stairs downwards, coming from small crystals set out like the night sky. Oddly enough to Ishtar, he recognised the constellations that were depicted there, it took him back to when he was a child. His father had taken him on one of his business trips to Australia. The roof looked like he was looking up at the night's sky over the equator.

Approaching the pedestal, Ishtar saw writing there along with a triangle shaped depression, clearly in the shape of the smoky black jewel that he had found earlier. Taking the jewel out of his inventory Ishtar placed it tip down into the depression and…. nothing happened.

"Of course it wouldn't be that easy," Ishtar mumbled to himself. Actually, reading what was written on the pedestal this time.

"The infinite and ever expanding
space is hers to command
She is all, but she is empty,
She is everywhere, but she is nowhere,
She is always, but out of time.

*She is the Goddess of Eternity and
Infinity and you are hers!
Bow before her majesty and
Name that which is above you."*

"Well I have absolutely no idea...shit," Ishtar exclaimed.

*

Half an hour later found Ishtar lying on the ground exasperated and staring up at the roof actually looking at the constellations trying to think what the riddle could be. After another five minutes staring at the exact same spot, Ishtar noticed some of the lights were slightly dimmer than the ones around them. Thinking back to when he enjoyed studying Astronomy before he started playing as many games as he did, Ishtar started to remember the names of the ones that were dimmer. Ishtar looked across the entire ceiling and saw that two were repeated.

"So that's Taurus, the next one is Hydra, I'm pretty sure that one is Ignis and the one after that is Aquarius…. hmmm I think that's Draco next, I have no idea about that one and Ignis again and finally Aquarius again." Ishtar went through them out loud.

"*Wait... above me? Those cheeky designers,*" Ishtar pondered, "*It's missing a character. So it's Thiad...ia. ...well I would think the missing character would be an* R." Ishtar thought immediately after, linking the initials of the constellations to the riddle.

Ishtar walked over to the pedestal, kneeled before it and loudly said: "I Kneel before the Lady Thiadria."

A bright light appeared as the Pyramid jewel fused into the pedestal, and the massive doors in front of him scraped open. Once again only a single pedestal was in the next room, this time there was a single red orb about the size of a golf ball sitting on the pedestal. Ishtar walked into the room, grabbed the Orb off the pedestal, and collapsed.

*

A female Naga sat upon a throne of bone made from those she had slaughtered. She smiled down at the entertainment at the foot of her primitive palace. The savages she conquered had just started to eat the captured ship crew alive. Just as the sun descended behind her, a Blue Orb appeared in her hand and the savages that could see her cringe.

*

A Wood Elf exited the woods where he had spent the last month. He'd been killing for his food and gaining levels. He had finally hit level fifty and could leave Undris for the Lost Continent, he turned his attention back to the Port City of Undaris in the distance.

This forest had changed his in-game life, between finding the hidden Wood Elf city and finding the mysterious temple in there too. With that, a Brown Orb appeared for an instant over his hand he kept walking towards the city.

*

A human in resplendent golden armour looking like the quintessential Paladin was standing on the foredeck of a Ship as the first sight of the middle continent came into view. A dark grey hulking Wolfman wearing leather armour and a Bow on his back approached the Paladin from behind.

"Are we even going to find a new dojo Eric? I want to keep training," he asks.

Immediately whipping around Eric backhands the Wolfman, "I told you to call me Justice while we are here. I will be the strongest and rule this world. My father assured me of that, after all, he told me how to get this armour." he snarled.

For an instant, his eyes flashed red and a Green Orb flickered over his hand, the Wolfman cowered away.

Chapter 14 – Temple of Who?

"Hello, little one" a distinctly feminine voice pronounced.

Ishtar snapped back into awareness in an instant, he found himself lying on the ground in what looked like a home office with a bookcase full of tomes behind a large wooden desk and a fireplace to his right giving off no heat. He sat up and looked at the occupant of the seat on the other side of the desk, it was a woman (he assumed) wearing a featureless black cloak covering all of their body that he could see.

Looking around a bit, Ishtar saw they were alone. Though he knew something strange was happening when he looked up and saw a field of stars. He looked back at the figure before stepping toward her and sat down in a padded seat to the side of the desk.

"Where am I?" he asked, "and who are you?" He continued before she could answer.

"You have touched one of my elemental orbs, and you ask who I am? What was once a symbol of my power over that world is now the key to the prison the other Gods have created for me. Though you are here in mind only, your body is still in my ancient temple's vault, that you shouldn't have even been able to enter. How did you do that by the way?" Thiadria responded with some heat in her tone.

Ishtar had a confused expression on his face for half of her mini-tirade, before it was replaced a look of stunned shock when he realised he had been talking to a hidden God of the world, and finally to intrigue when he imagined a quest was going to appear from this meeting.

"So that would mean you are Thiadria the Goddess of Eternity and Infinity? Wait, what do you mean by 'that world'? Well if you don't want people entering your vault, don't put the answer to your vault on the roof of the entrance!" Ishtar started babbling in excitement.

"Well, those aren't technically my domains. They were time and space, which is why I had the same abilities as the rest of the pantheon combined, though they were all stronger in their particular speciality. Haha, you caught that, did you? There are many worlds Ishtar, you only know a couple of them. There is a massive multiverse out there, and this is a small universe by any measure. The strength of the Gods is extreme in this world only, and it's why they were scared of my powers, since I restricted them from growing stronger." Thiadria answered.

"My last High priest, a High Elf known as Carrington, was power hungry it turns out. He betrayed me to the other Gods because I wouldn't give him part of my power to make him a Demigod. I thought he would forgive me for the refusal as he was of a long-lived race.

Unfortunately, I was wrong. To this day I still don't know what the Gods offered him to collect my Sacred Elemental Orbs together and to turn them into the keys of my prisons. Each of the Elemental Orbs were imbued with a small part of my power over a single element. Using their combined powers, the other Gods included the small part of my power in the Orbs to seal a large percentage of the world as well as myself away from the rest of the universe." Thiadria continued telling her story.

"Wow so is there any way for me to bring you back to this world?" Ishtar asked, angling to get a quest.

"That's what I hoped you would say Ishtar, it will be a trying experience, but I wish for you to collect my six Elemental Orbs together and take them to my first temple where the seal was created. You will be challenged as you are not the only person to receive this quest, there are already three others though, two are abusing the power they have received. I would prefer for a kind person to unite the Orbs and release me but as long as the quest is completed, I will rejoice." Thiadria replied.

The quest window appeared in front of Ishtar after she finished speaking.

__Legendary Quest Received!__
The exiled Goddess Thiadria has requested you find or take from your competitors the six Sacred Elemental Orbs, that each contain a portion of her power, and take them to her first temple to release the contained portion of the world and herself back into this universe.

Note: if completed you will change the face of the world.
Reward:
Unknown
Yes/No

Ishtar was surprised since this was the first time he had received the option to say yes or no to a quest. He quickly hit yes before he received several other notifications that he minimised for the time being.

"Thank you Ishtar, and good luck," Thiadria said as she made a motion of pushing in his direction, quickly Ishtar felt as if he was falling. Just as his vision went black again, Ishtar heard a whisper "Only my High Priest knew the name Thiadria, my followers knew me as Thia."

After Ishtar had disappeared from the room, Thiadria spoke aloud to herself "If you are the one to complete the quest, I'm sorry for what you will find out."

*

Ishtar arose from his slumber, realising he was still in the vault. Looking around he couldn't see the Orb anywhere, but he felt different somehow. Unsure of just how long he had been "unconscious" while speaking to Thiadria, just as he was about to start opening the windows he had earlier minimised, he heard a rumbling in the tunnel from behind him.

Ishtar stood up and walked over to the door only to see the tunnel on the other side of the vault entrance crumbling to the ground, blocking the passage back into the temple grounds.

"The Orb must have been holding this area together, though now how do I get out?" Ishtar mumbled to himself.

He hurried around the vault banging against the wall as hard as he could, he was actually losing little bits of health due to how hard he was hitting the stone of the walls. On the opposite side of the room from the door, he found what he was looking for, as soon as he hit the wall it popped open. Unfortunately, the room on the other side of the door was pitch black. Thinking how to solve the problem since it was still a few hours before he could summon Snow back

191

Ishtar looked at his abilities and found multiple new spells that he must have received from the Orb.

Using the new spell Fire Eyes Ishtar walked into the short tunnel he could now see perfectly. The tunnel was very short and at the end, was a set of spiral stairs twice as wide as the stairs he descended to arrive at the vault. Taking a deep breath, Ishtar took one final look back at the vault that had just changed the way he would play the game and started walking up the stairs.

As he was walking up the stairs, Ishtar started reflecting back on his relatively short time in Ariair so far. Compared to others who started at the same time as him his levelling rate has been quite slow but that was partially due to the hell-week he had spent with Quattra, he never regretted the training because he had gained extra stats from it. He hadn't really obtained any extra stats in a while, he just assumed he hadn't been doing the right things to gain them. On the other hand, he did gain an amazing companion in Snow, he still hated that he couldn't save her before. If it weren't for the ability to summon her back, he would have died a little inside.

He started to wonder what impact getting the Fire Orb would have considering it was supposed to be the opposite to his race, considering it came with a Legendary Quest, the faith of one of the former Gods of the world, and a true goal for his time in this world. It was when he noticed his thoughts heading in that direction that the utter realism of the world of Ariair was having him think less and less that he was playing a game, and more that he was truly in another world.

Since the Fire Eyes spells only lasted five minutes, Ishtar knew that he had been walking up the stairs for around a half hour before he found the top without looking at the time on the menu screen. Considering the distance, he assumed he was around the level of the entry floor of the mine he started in. Pushing against the stone directly ahead of him, Ishtar found it to be a clever one-way device, allowing him to exit but blocking anyone who wanted to enter from the other side.

As Ishtar pushed the stone he started seeing webs around the side, his anger instantly coming back.

"KILL THEM, SLAUGHTER THEM" Ishtar softly heard in his mind, his eyes went red in rage and his body started moving without his conscious thought.

A voice that was his but wasn't his spoke out, it was deeper and thick with malice,

"ARMAGEDDON"

The Fire Orb appeared above his outstretched hand and waves of flames started radiating around him into the sea of small spiders; two of the Black Blood Poisonspitters and one metallic one he hadn't seen before. Ishtar's rage kept increasing but it wasn't a normal rage, he felt like there was an oppressive blackness that was pressing down on him.

Somehow the spell kept going and going, Ishtar knew he shouldn't have enough mana regeneration to withstand using this spell for so long. He had seen this spell on his list, but since his class was Elemental Knight, he didn't think he would be able to use the spell very often. It wasn't how a normal Elemental Knight fought and its cooldown was huge.

Just as the last spider in the room died, his rage disappeared like it was never there. The blackness he felt weighing down on him before disappeared and he could finally move as he willed it again, instead of the rage being in control. His spell also stopped now he was back in control, but in those last few seconds before it finished it had depleted his entire mana pool.

The details of the battle were just added to the growing list of notifications that he was yet to check. Now that a large group of enemies were dead and he had escaped the hidden temple's vault, it was time to read through all those notifications finally.

Your pet Snow has died

You can summon her from the Spirit World after 24 hours have passed.

You have found a Temple hidden by Gods and Time
Your title 'Seeker of the Hidden' has increased to level two
+1 to all stats per title level

You have solved the puzzle to gain access to the Hidden Temple Vault and found the Sacred Elemental Orb of Fire
Your title 'Seeker of the Hidden' has increased to level three
+1 to all stats per title level

Through Godly powers, you have gained access to an element opposite to your races capability.
You can change your Race to Elemental Draconian to stop the opposite Elements from destroying your body slowly.
Would you like to change your race?
Yes/No

Congratulations you have gained a new Title
'Chosen of Thia'
+10% to all stats

You have been afflicted by the curse 'Rage of the Revenger'
A small part of the Goddess Thia's emotions at the other Gods and Goddesses has been infused into the Sacred Elemental Stone. The Sacred Elemental Stone of Fire has a portion of her great Rage. When your anger turns into Rage this curse will activate.

*The wielder is consumed by their Rage until death or the
complete eradication of their enemies.*
[Rage] Stat added
+500% Mana Regeneration

Ishtar touched the Rage stat to see what the details of it were.

Rage:
*A stat that increases per the owner's emotions. Once it reaches
a peak point the affiliated curse activates.*

You have successfully killed:
*Black Blood Poisonspitters x2
Black Blood Iron Carapace Spider x1
Black Blood Spiderlings x25
You have gained 2,975 Exp*

Ishtar was ecstatic at all the fantastic things he received from coming into this Mine and the new abilities and title he had received. Checking on the title Ishtar saw that 'Chosen of Thia' even stacked on top of the 'Seeker of the Hidden' title which makes it even better. Finally, he reopened the change of Race window and seeing no downside he clicked yes.

Almost immediately there was a sharp pain in his chest, and he collapsed.

"Not again," he said just as he hit the ground.

Chapter 15

For the third time that day Ishtar came awake on the floor not completely sure of anything that had happened, especially with his change in sub-race. He assumed it would have had a significant impact on his character, though he didn't immediately check his status or the new notifications awaiting him. What held his complete attention was the lack of timer for when he could summon Snow meaning it had ended while he was unconscious. He had spent the better part of the last day unconscious in the game for different reasons.

He quickly raised the command to bring her back. He missed her terribly. He had quickly grown attached to his adorable yet vicious companion. Using the summon ability that appeared when she became his pet, a small silver portal, perfectly sized for her height appeared near him, on the opposite side of the portal to him Snow stepped through.

Without turning to face him Snow started to "speak", her voice penetrating his mind, *"Master I'm so glad you are ok. I don't want to go back to that place though, it was dark and scary with all those other voices. I was lonely without you…"* Snow was turning around as she started talking to Ishtar and paused mid-word as she saw him, slightly jumping backwards in shock.

"*W-w-what happened to you M-m-master??*" Snow stuttered at Ishtar.

"What do you mean, Snow?" Ishtar responded.

"*You're all different looking.*" Snow explained.

Wanting to look at himself Ishtar wished he had a mirror and much to his surprise his magic responded to his thought and created a film of water before him reflecting his image. Even he was shocked at the changes to his body. No longer was he a shade of blue but a silvery white. There appeared to be no other superficial changes, though. Assuming some of the new notifications were about his bodily transformation, he decided to check them.

Your Race has changed from Water Draconian to Elemental Draconian
You have a 50% bonus to all Elemental damage.
As you are the first being to become an Elemental Draconian your racial and class bonuses are doubled.
+300 Fame

Wanting to finish this quest and get back to town, Ishtar started moving towards the only other opening in this cave; just to the right of the entrance tunnel which was opposite the stairs from where he had come. The tunnel curved around to the right, at its end was a small room. The room was notable for the oddly different feel it gave in comparison to the rest of the mine. For some reason, the oppressive air that had been pushing on his mind without him even knowing disappeared and he stood slightly straighter. A window popped up in the bottom right of his vision as opposed to the normal windows.

Well, that explained everything. Although on the other hand, Ishtar knew that whenever a safe place appeared in games it normally meant there was going to be a boss in the next room. Resting till he was at full Mana, Health and Stamina, Ishtar with Snow back by his side moved down the tunnel to the next room, not sure if he would be capable of killing what he found there. He knew he was getting closer because for the first time in the mine he could actually see a light coming from the end of the tunnel.

Ishtar slowly moved down the tunnel expecting to see something interesting. What he found at the other end of the tunnel was a dimly lit large circular room, as he stepped into the room part of the room lit up brighter. As Ishtar started to look up to see why only part of the room lit up a large form dropped from the roof, landing in the middle of the room.

Not that he would ever admit to anyone, but, Ishtar may have squealed like a little girl and jumped back into Snow as he realised it was a huge tarantula. The Blood Spider stood around three metres tall, with seemingly proportionally thicker armour. He immediately used Appraisal on the creature.

Black Blood Guardian
Type: Arachnid Level: 15

There is normally only one or two of these spiders per nest due to their size and their viciousness. They eat twenty times that of any other spider and kill any others that approach its size. Normally the Queen will have to separate them from the rest of the nest.

Ishtar was seeing just why this mission was supposed to be for a full party with tank, dps and healer. He was glad to see Appraisal had been steadily increasing in level to give more information. Ishtar knew he would have to take the role of all three with an amount of dps from Snow. First, he would have to explain the plan of engagement to her.

"Snow it will just be you and me in this fight, I will try to keep its attention on me. This is known as tanking and pulling aggro. I will Heal both of us as needed too, and finally if I do get too hurt I will need you to get its attention and run around the room. This is 'kiting'. I need you to remember these terms so during the battle or in future I can just tell you to do one of them you will know what I mean" Ishtar explained.

"OK master I will try to remember, so you just want me to attack it as much as possible then?" Snow asked.

"No, I will need to attack it first to get aggro before you do. Otherwise, it will focus on you instead of me" Ishtar replied. "Ok let's get this done Snow so we can go back to town and learn to craft." He started moving forwards.

They moved forwards together into the cave, Ishtar casting Stone Skin as he split from Snow moving to the opposite side of the Guardian.

"Remember Snow, don't attack until its entire attention is on me and as soon as it goes to attack me cast your Light Globe right in its eyes" Ishtar explained.

"*Yes, master.*" Snow absently responded as she circled to the other side of the Guardian.

As Ishtar moved within a short distance from the Guardian it finally seemed to notice him but still didn't move from where it was standing, he could see stairs leading downwards just behind it. He really didn't know what element the Guardian would be weak against, so he figured he would try all of them to see which did the most damage.

He first moved in to use his most powerful ability; Blades of Water. This was the first time he had actually used the ability. It was fantastic, his blade glowed blue and extended a metre as he was swinging at the spider's closest leg, scoring a clean hit that barely cut into its carapace. At the same time he was swinging, Snow created a Light Globe right in front of the Guardians eyes. As soon as Ishtar's sword hit the Guardian, it screamed and jumped to its left completely over Ishtar, one of its legs barely missing him as he brought his shield up in time and ducked.

Now that Snow and Ishtar were on the same side of the Guardian they had to be prepared to take whatever its next attack would be. Ishtar could have sworn that the Guardian was glaring at him from the other side of the room before it charged at him. Wanting to see whether he could take the charge Ishtar lowered his centre of gravity and activated Guard.

The Guardian, weighing substantially more than Ishtar, barrelled straight through him and stopped a short distance past where he had been standing. Ishtar, on the other hand, flew back into the nearby wall damaging himself. Fortunately for him, the Guard ability did its job and the only damage he took was the impact on the wall. Standing back up, Ishtar didn't bother healing himself since he hadn't taken much damage. He saw that Snow had attacked the Guardian's back after it had finished its charge at Ishtar and then moved away, the Guardian had started the same motions it had made before, charging again at Ishtar.

Ishtar knew he had played a game with a Boss similar to this one before, and just as it was starting its charge, Ishtar remembered why it was familiar and yelled to Snow.

"Snow, wait near the wall and once it has started moving jump to one side of where it is aimed," he instructed.

Snow looked at Ishtar for a moment before nodding at him, the Guardian charged Snow, who jumped out of the way. With an impact that rattled the entire room, the huge Guardian ran straight into the wall. Ishtar marvelled at the fact the Guardian couldn't stop before the wall and was stunned, it would appear that even this world followed general physics and that mass, once in motion, is very hard to stop if another force doesn't act upon it. It had been Ishtar's weight and Guard ability that robbed it of its speed the first time it had charged.

Knowing the simple strategy he could use to defeat the Guardian, this fight would become much easier. Ishtar was unsure of which element would be most effective against the Guardian, so he had to experiment. He attacked the Guardian first with a Lightning Shock to get its attention and have it charge at him again. After hitting the wall, it was again stunned for a short time before Ishtar cycled through all his other various elemental attacks to test. Blade of Water seemed to yield the most damage to the Black Blood Guardian, likely because it was his highest-level ability.

Now he had his strategy working Ishtar spent the next fifteen minutes whittling down the Guardian's health down to about 75% before the Guardian changed. Its cracked outer exoskeleton broke apart and Ishtar saw a dull grey spider crawl out of the opening. The second spider quickly darkened in colour, resembling that of the original. This newly moulted Guardian was a bit smaller than before but appeared to be faster.

With the faster Guardian, it became harder for Ishtar and Snow to dodge its charges, but they were still fast enough to do so. It took another half hour to continue their strategy and get the Guardian down to 50%, when it once again moulted, becoming smaller and faster. Once again Snow and Ishtar were fast enough to avoid most of the faster charges, but were getting hit every now and then, using up a decent amount of Ishtar's mana using his Minor Heal to keep them in good health.

Finally, an hour later they finally got the Guardian down to a quarter of its health, but that was when everything went to hell. This time when the Guardian moulted it was barely taller than Ishtar himself and instead of charging at Snow, who had its attention, it shot a net of webbing that pinned her to the wall. It immediately leapt across the room at her, but Ishtar refused to see her die again. Ishtar started running at full speed across the room after the spider and threw both his Ice Dagger and his Mana Bolt at the left side of the Guardian hoping the impact would push it far enough away from Snow to prevent it from hurting her.

Ishtar was scared for her and for the first time, he noticed in the bottom corner of his vision a small display that was constantly increasing in small increments. Currently, it read 150. He assumed it was his Rage Counter. Fortunately, his desperate gambit moved the Guardian just enough to cause it to hit the wall, doing decent damage to itself rather than Snow. With it stunned, Ishtar had enough time to cut Snow out of the web so that they could both retreat away from the Guardian. They were halfway across the chamber and splitting up as the Guardian shook itself and stood back up turning to face them.

Knowing that the Guardian would now shoot a web net caused Ishtar to try to concentrate as hard as he possibly could even though he was mentally worn out from how long the fight had gone. Before Ariair, all the games he had played had either been on consoles or using the keyboard on his PC, it took so much more concentration when he had to move his body instead of just pushing buttons.

Ishtar started to dodge as he saw the Guardian jump in his direction, taking two steps to the side of where the Guardian was aimed. He was waiting for the shooting of its web and just as the Guardian was at the peak of its jump, it shot out its web at him. Even knowing it was coming, Ishtar was almost hit and covered by the web. He immediately dashed forward to attack the creature with his two most powerful abilities before it could land. His blade glowed Red on the downstroke as he activated Cleave hammering the lighter and less armoured Guardian into the ground and then as he spun to deliver a full force upstroke. The blade went Blue and grew with Blades of Water, doing more damage in a single combo than any five attacks had before the last moulting. He finally had the Guardian down to 10% as he retreated, the Guardian once again standing up.

"Snow let's finish this. Flare your Light Globe into its eyes and let's kill it." Ishtar yelled as he turned away.

A bright flash appeared for a brief moment behind Ishtar before he turned back around to see the Guardian stumbling around randomly on its limbs. Ishtar and Snow moved from either side of it to attack. Ishtar nodded to Snow who then charged in and used her Light Claw on the Guardian's face, scoring a critical hit and taking it down to 8% before Ishtar moved in to repeat his last combo of Cleave and Blades of Water. The Guardian was barely moving after the punishing attacks, but still had a sliver of Health left, so Ishtar used a Quick Thrust into its brain to finish it off. He then immediately collapsed onto the ground next to an equally tired Snow before even looting the Guardian's body.

Your party has successfully killed the floor boss
Black Blood Guardian x1
You have gained 15,000 Exp each

Ishtar gained one level, while Snow gained four from the end of that battle. It took them so long of a time at their relatively low levels, that they could have gained more from fighting normal mobs outside of the dungeon. Due to the gains for Snow, Ishtar checked her status and used her free stats to increase her magic and speed.

Status
Name: *Snow*
Race: *Light Wolf*
Level: 9
Experience: *250/9000*
Health: *220/220*   **Health Regen:** *5.4/ Sec*
Mana: *260/260*   **Mana Regen:** *9.0/ Sec*
Stamina: *190/190*   **Stamina Regen:** *20.0/ Sec*
-

Strength: *26*   **Dexterity:** *20*
Agility: *29*   **Endurance:** *19*
Vitality: *22*   **Intelligence:** *26*
Wisdom: *12*   **Luck:** *10*
Free Stat Points: *0*

After resting for a further twenty minutes, Ishtar finally got around to looting the Guardian.

***Loot Menu**
2G
2x Light Stone
2x Minor Health Potion
Heart Shaped Stone
Take all Yes/No

It seemed the loot scaled depending on the members of the party, though Ishtar was surprised he didn't get any gear from such a powerful, essentially boss creature. However, he was curious about the Heart Shaped Stone, so he used Appraisal on it.

Chara Sanguis
Type: *Item* ***Durability:*** *Unbreakable*
Quality: *Unique*
A solidified piece of Blood and Bone from the Black Blood Spider Queen: Chara gave to her favoured child to evolve it into a Black Blood Guardian. Only one can be created by a Spider Queen every 10 Years.

Unsure of the use of the Chara Sanguis, Ishtar decided to head down to the next level of the cavern. He was after all still short for the amount of Iron he needed to complete his quest.

Chapter 16 – Caught in a Web

Ishtar and Snow made it to the next level, walking into an empty room with a torch on the wall and a tunnel across from them. With nowhere else to go and having recovered before leaving the Guardian room, Ishtar started towards the tunnel activating his Fire Eyes. With his new ability Snow no longer needed to use Light Globe for him to see since she could see in the dark.

At the end of the tunnel was a small room covered in webbing. There were two exits that Ishtar could see. The one to his left looked into a single massive cavern where he assumed the boss was waiting for him, so he led Snow into the other opening in the wall.

A short walk through another tunnel later, Ishtar and Snow found a cavern that appeared rougher than the others they had been through. As if this was the last area that had been carved out before the Mine had shut down and the Spiders had moved in. There were four Level fourteen-sixteen Black Blood Spiders near the entrance. Ishtar had Snow flank around the closest before using her Light Claw on the legs of the first one, just outside the aggro range of the other three so they could focus on the single one. Moving in as the Spider turned towards Snow, Ishtar used Cleave targeting the legs closest to him scoring a critical hit and cutting off two of the four legs and taking the Spider down to 30% health and taking the aggro back onto himself before Snow used her Light Claw on the Spider's eyes killing it.

Ishtar knew he and Snow could easily defeat these Spiders, so instead of trying to kill them. Ishtar decided to grind some of his abilities that he hadn't used as much. He decided to initiate the attack on the next Spider by casting Wind Strike and Quick Thrust at the same time into the Spider's face before immediately activating his Shield Bash to stun it.

His combo used up a lot of his Stamina and Mana, using the two at the same time doubled the cost of each. It took the Spider down to 35% Health and stunned it for two seconds, allowing Snow to attack with her Light Claw before ripping out the throat of the Spider. The other two Spiders that were there were killed the same way. Ishtar then quickly looted the bodies for some Spider Pieces before moving on.

The cavern was the size of a football field and curved to the left the deeper he went into the room. Just at the junction where the cavern turned stood one of the Black Blood Iron Carapace. Since it had a much higher defence and he didn't currently have any offensive fire spells that he could use at his level, Ishtar knew he would need to plan this fight. The last Iron Carapace he killed was while he was under the influence of the Rage curse.

Having to tank the Spider Ishtar cast Stoneskin on himself before advancing towards it, to gain aggro Ishtar shot his Mana Bolt and cast his Ice Dagger before unsheathing his sword. He guessed he had gained the Iron Carapace Spider's full attention since it immediately rushed him, striking him with its front leg while Ishtar activated Guard and took the hit. Ishtar was knocked back a couple of metres, the Spider broke his Guard ability but didn't do much damage. Neither the Mana Bolt nor Ice Dagger had done much damage, leading Ishtar to believe that the Iron Carapace Spider was all defence and very little attack, only using its size and weight for Knockback attacks. It would be a deadly combination if any Poisonspitter Spiders were supporting one of them.

Almost immediately the Iron Carapace Spider charged to attack Ishtar again, so Ishtar used Cleave aiming to hit the leg that was coming towards his torso. The two attacks clashed between them, a loud crack was heard, and Ishtar's sword bounced back from the spider. Stepping back, Ishtar used the motion of his sword bouncing back to turn, increasing the speed of his strike. He used his Lightning Shock, hoping to take advantage of the conductivity of Iron.

Much to Ishtar's pleasure he managed to hit the same place of the Spider's front leg as his Cleave and not only did the Iron of the Carapace conduct the Lightning Element, but his Cleave had cracked the outer Carapace. The small discharge component of the attack broke the Carapace even more while causing about 15% damage. The Iron Carapace Spider slumped to the ground after the attack, while its legs were slightly spasming. This caused Ishtar to believe using Lightning Shock caused a Stun effect. Just as it slumped down Snow came from behind it, activating her Light Claws and performing what Ishtar assumed was a Light-imbued Bite, which created large scratches and a small amount of damage but did not break the Carapace.

After seeing how easily the Iron Carapace Spider succumbed to Stun effect from his Lightning Shock, Ishtar only used normal attacks doing minimal damage while renewing the Stun whenever the Spider went to stand back up. This quickly brought the Iron Carapace Spider down to the red zone of its health. Then Ishtar stepped back to give the kill to Snow, who had been doing more damage than Ishtar by attacking the breaks in its Carapace.

You have successfully killed:
Black Blood Iron Carapace Spider x1
Your Pet Snow inflicted the final blow
She has gained 400 Exp

Ishtar even got ten pieces of Black Blood Iron as loot from the Iron Carapace Spider. He had no idea what changes the Spider's influence would have on the Iron, but he was sure it would be better than standard Iron in the game. Moving deeper into the cavern Ishtar found another small Iron deposit in the wall gaining another fifteen Pieces of Ore, he only needed another ten Pieces of Ore to make up the fifty Pieces the quest needed.

Ishtar kept walking through the Cavern, and he could now see the end. Unfortunately, there was a bulkier version of a Black Blood Spider with claw-tipped front legs near the wall, with a small chest on the ground and the glint of ore in the wall behind it. Ishtar again used Appraisal,

Black Blood Spider [Elite]
Type: Arachnid Level: 20
One of the Elite protectors of a Black Blood Spider nest

As Ishtar advanced towards the Elite Spider, he heard the tell-tale *SPIT* of a Poisonspitter from just inside an alcove that he couldn't see around an outcropping. He quickly tried jumping back attempting to dodge the attack. Unfortunately, he was still hit on the chestplate with a bit splashing onto his shoulder, reducing his health and the durability of his Chestplate almost to breaking point. He was only hoping it lasted until he got back to River City and received the repair ability.

A flash of Silver greeted Ishtar's eyes as Snow sprinted past him to attack the Poisonspitter Spider, using Flash on its eyes to blind it, followed by a Light Claw and a regular swipe of her claws across its face, getting a critical hit and taking over half its health away. Ishtar stepped in stabbing it through the head using Quick Strike before activating Blades of Water and immediately finishing it off.

Ishtar realised he was lucky he was walking near the wall after finding that ore, otherwise he imagined the Poisonspitter would have attacked them from behind in a spectacularly efficient ambush mid-fight with the Elite Spider. Assuming there would be the same ambush point on the other side of the cavern Ishtar circled the area in a big loop, so he didn't enter the aggro range of the Elite Spider. As he had Snow approach, since she was much faster than him, they both heard the tell-tale *Spit* sound of its attack. Snow quickly dodged the ranged attack and used Flash to blind the Poisonspitter, following that up by attacking its face. Ishtar was closely following, using a different combo of stabbing it with Quick Thrust then activating Wind Strike, which exploded out of the Poisonspitter's head.

Ishtar and Snow rested to recover Mana and Stamina before heading towards the Black Blood Spider [Elite]. He may have highly enhanced stats for his level due to his titles and extra training he had done, but even with Snow, he assumed he would have trouble with an Elite Mob that was five levels above him.

Activating Stone Skin to increase his defence and ready to activate Guard at a moment's notice Ishtar wanted to gauge the speed and strength of this

Elite. He started by firing a Mana Bolt at it, dealing very little damage to its thicker carapace but still causing the Elite take notice of him, charging straight at Ishtar. Ishtar activated Guard and bent his knees planning on taking the hit, shortly after the Elite solidly collided with his Shield, though it wasn't heavy or strong enough to push Ishtar back. Ishtar responded with a Shield Bash, but the Elite was immune to both the Knockback and the Stun effect.

While that was happening, Snow had circled around the back of the Elite and let loose a pair of Light Claws at its back getting a Critical Hit on the joint of its rear leg. The Elite spun and slammed into Snow knocking her back and doing 40% damage, such was its immense strength. Ishtar threw a heal on her quickly before attacking the same leg that Snow had with Cleave, opening up the scratch Snow had created. He quickly used Guard when the Elite spun back at him, slamming into his Shield with its claw and doing decent damage even through Guard. Ishtar topped up Snow's health with another Minor Heal before healing himself a bit, while he was doing that Snow repeated her last attack. She once again hit the same place on the Elite as it focused on Ishtar, though this time when it turned towards her, she jumped back away from the attack.

The leg that Ishtar and Snow had been attacking had been bleeding fairly heavily and the Elite had stopped putting weight on it, so instead Ishtar instructed Snow to swap to the other leg.

Within four revolutions of the Elite going back and forth between Snow and Ishtar, it was unable to use either back leg which slowed it considerably while taking its health down to 30%.

As the Elite's health neared 25%, Ishtar worried that it would have a Berserk ability or something similar. He next used Cleave since he was running low on mana. He kept both his and Snow's health up and managed to cut off the Elite's leg by getting a Critical Hit. This dropped the Elite down to 10% health while inflicting a Heavy Bleeding status effect. With both the bleeding of the wounds, along with their strategy, the Elite was dead shortly after. Both Ishtar and Snow slumped to the ground as soon as it died.

You have successfully killed:
Poisonspitter Spiders x2
Black Blood Spider [Elite] x1
You have gained 1700 Exp

"Jeez I really should have listened when they said this was a Dungeon for a full team, though I'm way stronger than when I got here aren't I Snow?" Ishtar exclaimed.

"*I guess Master, will people recognise you with your new look?*" Snow responded.

"Huh I didn't think of that…I'm gonna have to avoid telling anyone anything about the Orb so I will have to figure out a way to explain my look away...Wait, you don't think the City Lord knew the Orb was here with the "extra payment for unique items" on the quest paperwork?" answered Ishtar.

Snow not knowing how to answer Ishtar kept quiet and moved away to look around the area. Ishtar went to the wall where he saw the unknown ore and tried to use Appraisal on it.

****UNKNOWN****

Your Appraisal level isn't high enough to Appraise this item

Ishtar went at the Ore deposit with his Pickaxe anyway and came away with twenty-five pieces of the silvery-gold metal. With another Ore deposit to the side, he obtained the final ten Pieces of Iron Ore he needed for the Quest. Now he could check the chest and then go look in that other room before leaving. In the chest, he found a Gnarled Branch with a thumb-sized Emerald secured to the top. He used Appraisal on it before placing it in his Inventory.

Nymph Staff
Type: *Staff* ***Durability:*** *80/80*
Quality: *Rare* ***Damage:*** *10-15*
A Wizard's staff made from the remains of a Nymph's Tree home.
+15 to Intelligence
+ 25% Damage to Earth and Nature Spells

A Staff that was cool, but absolutely useless to him, so Ishtar planned to sell it in the auctions when he got back to town. Ishtar walked back across the cavern and made his way back through to the start, tentatively walking into the other cavern. He was confused as he couldn't see any enemies. Though the wall was covered in web-like shapes that looked an awful lot like people, he walked over to the closest one and used his sword to cut it open. Inside he found the deteriorated remains of a Draconian. Slightly scared and repulsed, Ishtar stepped back and slowly moved further into the cavern with his head rotating, looking for any enemies. Just as he and Snow reached the middle of the cavern, a net of web was dropped from the ceiling completely sealing both his and Snow's movement. With his Rage stat slowing rising, the darkened area to the back of the cavern lifted its veil to reveal a giant Arachne with five Black Blood Spider [Elite] surrounding it.

"You invade my home and kill my Children, Adventurer. What reassson do you have to do so?" The Arachne hissed at Ishtar.

Ishtar used Appraisal on the Arachne before answering.

Black Blood Spider Queen: Chara
Type: *Arachne* ***Level:*** *25*
A newly evolved Arachne with an Affinity for Dark Magic that has taken over the Miditarac Iron Mine for its abnormal level of Mana in the environment

"How the hell is this supposed to be a possible quest for even a party of three?" Ishtar thought to himself.

"I was given a Quest from River City to help reopen this Iron Mine by removing the Spiders. Since they have all attacked me, I assumed that I was meant to kill them all." Ishtar answered knowing there was no way in hell he could win this fight and his only way out was to talk fast. His Rage stat had stopped increasing as he lost his anger at being trapped, and he started to despair about being unable to match the Power before him.

"The only reasssson I have not fed you to my children already is you smell different to most who have come before and alssso of my Ssssaaanguiss that I want back," Chara responded.

"Well is there any chance if I give it back you will let me go? Also, I can guarantee if I die, even more, powerful people will come to kill you. I could always lie and say I killed you all if you move your nest?" Ishtar appealed to her hoping like hell that she would accept.

"I can always take my Sssanguiss from your corssspe, my little morsel" Chara mocked Ishtar

"That's where you're wrong Queen Chara. I'm a Traveller and will be reborn with nearly everything I own. You would be taking a risk killing me while I still have your Chara Sanguis." Ishtar partially lied since it was a Dungeon specific item he would probably drop it. He removed it from his inventory and showed it to her as he said it.

"Fine! Give me what issss mine and in return, I will not kill you!" Chara almost hissed at Ishtar.

A small Black and Green spider climbed up the web to Ishtar's hand and carried over the Chara Sanguis to its Queen. Ishtar felt another small spider climb up onto his neck and a small prick at his neck. Immediately starting to feel drowsy Ishtar slowly collapsed into the web around him believing he had been betrayed. Just before his consciousness was completely lost, he heard Chara speak once more.

"Thank you for your warning little morssssel, the mana has been getting weaker anyway so we ssshall leave to find a new home."

Chapter 17

Ishtar woke to find a still unconscious Snow on the ground next to him just outside of the Mine. The alert for notifications blinked at him.

"Getting really tired of being knocked out or falling unconscious in this game" he muttered as he stood up.

He decided to check his notifications before heading back to town.

You have been poisoned.
Due to your low poison resistance, you have lost consciousness

Skill Learnt:
Minor Poison Resistance Beginner level 1
Well done, you have survived being poisoned. How proud of yourself you must be.

Ishtar couldn't help but think there were multiple "Gods" writing the Notifications since some seemed factual, but others were almost mocking or bitchy. He wasn't sure whether to laugh or groan, much like how he felt whenever one of his friends were on a Pun rampage. Not sure how long it was going to be until Snow woke up Ishtar decided not to wait so picked her up and started walking back to the City.

They were almost back to the City before Snow woke up. It got to the point that Ishtar had started to worry about her. Yet, as she had full health he knew there was nothing that he could actually do. Fortunately, his worries were alleviated when she woke up. The rest of the walk back to River City was spent in silence as Ishtar deliberated on what he would say if anyone asked about his change in body colour. The best plan he had come up with so far was declaring that he didn't know, basically the worst excuse ever.

The walls of the City finally came into view, spurring Ishtar and Snow into a jog. Within fifteen minutes they were just entering the gates. Being waved through the gate with a quick show of his Adventurers card, Ishtar was surprised when a hand came down onto his shoulder.

"Good to see you are growing fast and have already discovered your second Element lad, though I can't tell what it is from your colouring." Ishtar turned to find Captain Kieras beaming at him.

"Oh, hello Captain, how have you been? umm, Air and Water now" Ishtar replied after a quick pause to quickly think of an Affinity that would explain his change.

"Same old, same old lad. Gates need guarding; I am in charge of them all after all. Good form. Air and Water are a good mix. Why don't you come get a Beer at the tavern with some of us tonight, I know you don't really know anyone in town, plus a new Affinity should always be celebrated!" Kieras replied with a hearty chuckle.

"I'd like that, thank you. I just need to go hand in a few quests. Where should I meet you?" Ishtar said while relaxing now he knew he didn't need to come up with an excuse for his new look.

"Me and the boys finish our shift at sunset so meet us at the Leaping Fool just down the street from the Adventurers Guild about then," Kieras answered.

"See you then," Ishtar said as he walked away towards the Guards Barracks to give all the Ore to Coal.

*

Ishtar walked into the Smithy to the roaring of fire and the constant ringing of hammer meeting metal. Not wanting to interrupt Coal, Ishtar stepped to the side and just watched for the next ten minutes. The seamless movement of a man who had done the same task hundreds of times was almost mesmerising to watch. Coal appeared completely absorbed in his work and within twenty minutes of Ishtar watching turned a bar of metal into a dagger that curved backwards as it tapered to its point with the edge only on the outside curve of the blade.

It was once he had quenched the blade in the bucket of oil to the side that Coal finally looked up towards Ishtar and spoke.

"Like my Dirk, do you Ishtar?"

"Didn't even know what kind of blade it was honestly, I only came to bring you Ore from the Miditarac Iron Mine to get the repair book from you," Ishtar replied.

"It's a duellist's blade used in the offhand instead of a shi…Wait for WHAT! Did you go to that cursed place? Do you have any idea how many miners have been killed by the different monsters that continuously gravitate to that place? As soon as someone killed the monsters there, another group appeared in the month!" Coal yelled at Ishtar.

"There was a quest from the City to clear out the spiders that were there, so I did both at the same time. I was told the Mana density was reducing there so monsters probably won't be as much of a problem anymore." Ishtar responded.

"That's good, we can finally stop buying all our Iron from Cindera like we have been doing. With all the Volcanoes in the area it's a dangerous place to mine for anyone other than Fire Draconians, it does have the highest quality of Ore in the country though." Coal replied.

Ishtar walked over to an empty bin and nodded towards it while looking at Coal indicating that he wanted to put the Iron Ore in there, Coal nodded his consent, so Ishtar dropped most of it in, keeping only the Black Blood Iron and the mystery metal. Hoping to gain something extra for the rare metals, Ishtar wouldn't show them to Coal until after he got the Quest Completion.

Coal walked over to inspect the bin and sorted through the ore putting them in multiple different bins across the workshop, how he was sorting them was a mystery to Ishtar. When he had finished sorting, he left the room into what appeared to be an office. A short time later he exited the office with a book in hand and walked up to Ishtar.

"Looks like you got me what I requested. Here is the spell book for Repair" Coal stated as he handed the book to Ishtar.

Quest Completed! – Blacksmith's Request
You have collected the 50 Pieces of Ore for the Blacksmith Coal
Reward:
Skill Book: Repair

"Thank you" Ishtar responded as he quickly used the skill book to get Repair.

Repair:
A spell that gives you the ability to Repair equipment with your Mana. At low levels, a loss of Durability will be in effect.
Cost: 50 Mana per Cast

Ishtar immediately used his new Repair spell on his chestplate to find out how much it actually repaired. A blinding white light flashed all over his chest, once Ishtar could see again, Ishtar saw that some of the scratches and dents had disappeared. To see the difference Ishtar used Appraisal on his Chestplate.

Bronze Chestplate
Type: *Chestplate* **Durability:** *9/29*
Quality: *Basic* **Defence:** *5 (10)*
A heavily damaged basic Bronze Chestplate

Ishtar saw that it had repaired it about five points of Durability but had reduced the Max Durability by one. So, because he currently had 775 Mana left Ishtar used Repair on his Chestplate, Helmet and one of his Armguards before he ran out of Mana and had to wait. After he had done that much, he rechecked his Chestplate.

Bronze Chestplate
Type: *Chestplate* **Durability:** *24/26*
Quality: *Basic* **Defence:** *10*
A basic Bronze Chestplate

Now that he had to wait till his Mana Regenerated, he went back to talk to Coal who had gone back to work while Ishtar had been repairing his gear.

"Oh, by the way Coal, I found some other Ore while I was in the Mine. One called Black Blood Ore that came from a Metal Covered Spider and this other one I couldn't identify." Ishtar called out as he withdrew the other ores out of his inventory and put it in the bin his Iron ore had just been removed from.

Coal walked over and looked into the bin and flinched before slowly reaching in and grabbing the Black Blood Iron and looking back at Ishtar.

"This is some pretty interesting Ore lad, very Mana rich since it came from a monster. It's surprisingly flexible." Coal answered.

He then reached back into the bin and picked up a small piece of the other ore.

"I have absolutely no idea how you managed to get some of the rarest ore in the country though...This beautiful son of a bitch is called Electrum. A mana-rich mix of gold and silver, it's stronger than steel and is more mana conductive than pure silver, it's the perfect combination of the two and almost impossible to find." Coal declared.

Ishtar gained a grin as Coal spoke, "So it's valuable then? How about you make me a new set of Armour and I will give you the Black Blood Iron and Electrum?" he asked Coal.

"Lad, for this amount of these two ores I will make you a full set of Armour, have it completely enchanted and give you 250G. I refuse to cheat you on such an expensive Ore, the Armour made from the Black Blood Iron and Electrum and enchanting would cost 1000G plus I will have some left over for my own uses. It's going to take two days to create." Coal declared

"Thank you for being honest with me, Coal. I really appreciate it. I will come back in two days for the Armour. Then I will probably be leaving the City." Ishtar replied and left towards the Adventurers Guild.

*

Ishtar arrived at the Guildhall and went straight up to the counter to turn in his quest before going to meet Captain Kieras at the tavern since it was getting close to sundown. There was a pretty human woman behind the guild's counter.

"Hi, I would like to turn in a Quest," Ishtar started.

"Oh hello Adventurer, please either give me proof of completion or place your hand on this orb," she replied while pulling a crystal ball out from under the counter.

Ishtar nodded and put his hand on the ball, he was confused since he hadn't done this last time.

"So this ball will verify whether you are lying about clearing the mission or not. We just had it repaired, some adventurers don't like it when we tell them no. What was the mission you undertook?" She explained.

"I thought all this was recorded already and that I could just give you my guild badge? But anyway, I completed the Clear the Abandoned Mine quest." Ishtar replied as the crystal ball shone a dim green.

"Oh yes I need your Guild Badge too, sorry this is my first week working for the Guild. The ball detects no lie from you, but I've never seen it so dim before, it must be running out of Mana. We will need to have a Scout verify that the Mine has been cleared of Spiders before awarding the Quest to you. It will take up to a few hours, if you are okay with waiting here or on the tavern side? Oh, the Quest was also upgraded to a C -Rank Quest while you were gone due to the number of Adventurers who took it and never came back." the Receptionist answered.

"What! that's insane, I'm just gonna sit down." Ishtar finished as he became a little shaken considering Chara could have killed him at any time, he wasn't surprised by how many Adventurers had died.

*

An hour came and went very quickly for Ishtar since he was gazing blankly at a wall considering how badly he had screwed up by trying such a difficult quest alone with Snow. He had a hard time and came out much stronger, but he should never have risked Snow, he could have lost her forever as far as he knew at the time. He knew he was just lucky things had happened as they had.

"Ishtar!" a yell of his name brought Ishtar back to the present to see the receptionist motioning him back over to the counter.

"Hey sorry, was in another place," Ishtar said as he got up to the counter.

"We have had confirmation that the Miditaric Mines are now clear of any Spiders and you have officially been awarded the completion of the Quest. Due to the Quest being upgraded after you had taken it you will be given the upgraded Reward and also moved up two ranks in the Guild to 'D' Rank. To advance any further you will need to complete the tests involved. Can I help you with anything else?"

the receptionist finished as she handed Ishtar a small sack.

"No thank you. I will be leaving now, have a good night" Ishtar answered as he walked away and checked his latest notification.

Quest Completed
Clear the Abandoned Mine
C Rank Group Quest
Even though you didn't kill them all, you somehow managed to fluke this shit out and complete a Quest that should have killed you. I hope you enjoy your Rewards, cheater haha.
Reward:
15G
15000 Exp
1 Spell Book: Blink

Realising he was probably late Ishtar quickly asked a passer-by where the Leaping Fool was and found out it was actually pretty close, just about a hundred metres down the street. It didn't take Ishtar very long to make his way there only to find out he really was late; the Captain and a group of guards were already taking up the back half of the room spread across three tables. They were all greedily watching a rotating boar over a roaring fire.

It certainly smelt good Ishtar thought as he walked over.

Just before he made it to the table, Kieras saw him and greeted him.

"Hey Lad, good to see you could make it. Boys we have a little celebration tonight. Young Ishtar here discovered his second Affinity today, so the first few rounds are on me!" The news caused all the Guards to 'cheers' their Captain and crowd around Ishtar clapping him on the back as they forced him into a chair at the centre table across from Captain Kieras. It didn't take long before Ishtar found a slab of boar and a tankard of beer on the table in front of him. Being regaled with, mostly lies, stories from the guards around him. The banter between the men and women of different races made him miss playing with his friends, playing alone was feeling less and less fun without someone to have a joke with.

Eventually, Ishtar had a few beers and climbed up onto the table and started telling the story of his time in the Mines, naturally minus any information about the Temple of Thia. Just as he was midway through telling them about the Black Blood Guardian the door of the Leaping Fool burst open and ten Draconians in Ornate Armour marched in the door and up to the table, Ishtar was standing on.

"Ishtar, your presence has been requested by Lord Doorakian immediately." the obvious Leader announced.

Captain Kieras stepped forward, "What the hell do you want, Phillip? Can't you see the lad has had a few drinks, the Lord can wait until tomorrow."

"Kieras, get the hell out of our way. You are just a mere Gate Captain. Do what I say!" Phillip responded before nodding at some of his men who stepped forwards and dragged Ishtar off the table.

It wasn't until they were partly out the door before Ishtar could look back to see that Captain Kieras and the other Guards were being held at sword point by six of the Lord's Guards.

Chapter 18 – Meeting with the Lord

Within five steps, Ishtar got tired of being dragged. The fresh, cold air had cleared his mind, but he was affected by the systems mimicking the effects of alcohol. He slammed his left foot into the ground to unbalance the Lord's Guards dragging him, but in doing so, he also fell to the ground. The experience of fighting the Black Blood Spiders engaged his muscle memory, and he rolled to his side and bounced back to his feet before turning back to the group surrounding him.

Seeing that the six that had been holding the Gate Guards at sword point had re-joined the group around him and they were now all holding their swords, Ishtar held out his hands and tried to be unthreatening,

"I'd prefer to walk myself thanks, no need to drag me."

The leader who Captain Kieras had called Phillip, with a smirk, replied, "And what would you be able to do if we just kill you for the effort I had to put in coming down to this shitty area of town when I should be comfortably in my office in the castle?"

"Well since I am a Traveller I would revive at the temple. I then would be forced to tell your Lord that you killed an unarmed man and delayed him in talking to me. All because you got pissy because Kieras was with me," Ishtar answered trying to keep a straight face after seeing the obvious hatred the two men had for each other.

A look of pure rage immediately appeared on Phillips' face before he charged at Ishtar. He was intercepted by one of his men who quietly, just at the edge of Ishtar's hearing said,

"Sir remember what happened last time, if you lose your temper and he finds out again, you will get demoted to the Gate and then that bastard wins."

Ishtar filed this information away for later noticing this Draconian had some major anger issues he could potentially leverage. There was clearly a whole lot more history between him and Kieras that Ishtar wanted to find out.

"I will have to ask Kieras next time I see him," Ishtar thought to himself.

As if he had just seen something he liked, Phillip looked past Ishtar and smiled before chuckling, suddenly Ishtar felt a heavy impact and a splitting pain in the back of his head. As he fell to the ground, Ishtar looked up to see the smug Lord's Guard that had just hit him with the pommel of his sword.

Ishtar for the fourth time that day passed out.

*

Ishtar came back to awareness slowly. The first thing he noticed was his knees dragging along the ground, the muffled voices of his kidnappers surrounding him. As he looked up all he could see was the Castle in the middle of the City as they entered the gate.

His headache had not gone away, so he assumed it hadn't been long since they knocked him out. He did see new notifications though.

You have sustained a Concussion
-20 Intelligence for 6 hours

"Shit, not only are they stronger than me, but I still have a killer headache and my magic is weaker for the rest of the time I'm playing today too." Ishtar complained to himself as he tried to stand up instead of being dragged.

The Lord's Guards jolted in surprise, not knowing he had woken. The two that had been dragging him just let go and stepped back, not knowing if he would try to attack them.

Rather than do anything Ishtar put his arms out to his sides, palms up in a non-threatening manner and spoke,

"I'm not going to run or fight or anything. I never wanted trouble, so let's go see your Lord."

Phillip sneered at Ishtar but motioned away seven of his men, only keeping two. He pointed towards the door on the side of the castle that they were standing next to, not giving Ishtar the chance to look around.

Phillip opened the door and entered first, followed by Ishtar with the two remaining Lord's Guards trailing him.

The passage behind the door seemed to be disused or at least barely maintained, *"Probably servant passages, the Lord doesn't seem to care about the lower class"* Ishtar thought to himself.

They were deeper into the Castle through the cramped passages and up a flight of stairs before entering a proper hallway on what Ishtar assumed was the west side of the Castle. Immediately across the hallway from the passage was a single door that Phillip led Ishtar towards.

Following Phillip into the room Ishtar saw that it was a grandly appointed Study with a large Mahogany-coloured desk, multiple bookcases full of books, artwork and a statue on the walls to his right, and directly behind the desk was a large window overlooking River City and the River.

Seated behind the desk was quite possibly the smallest and skinniest Black Draconian Ishtar had ever seen. Looking at the almost wizened Draconian, Ishtar felt fear for the first time ever in the game. It was almost an Aura around this man, an Aura of Death. When he looked up, Ishtar saw that his eyes were the pure black of the void, and that void covered the whole eye. Upon seeing Ishtar, a grin appeared on Lord Doorakian's face, a smile that chilled Ishtar down to his bones. He stared at Ishtar for what felt like an eternity, before turning to Phillip.

"Captain, I think I will be okay alone with our friend here, you can take your men and have the rest of the evening off." the dark Draconian said.

"But my Lord he tried to escape and was violent to my men. He may try to attack you!" Phillip answered while standing at attention in front of Ishtar.

Ishtar deciding, he didn't like Phillip, so figured he could piss him off and potentially get him in trouble spoke up.

"I would have come willingly if you had asked, rather than ordered before getting into an argument with Captain Kieras before I could even respond. Especially since your men dragged me off the table and knocked me out when I tried to stand up."

In response to Ishtar's statement, much to his surprise, Lord Doorakian laughed and looked back to Ishtar.

"I don't care how he got you here; I order, and he follows. He's a loyal pet of mine. Phillip, next time try not to get into an argument with that man again. Next time you two fight in the street or a tavern I will demote you both. I will not have you tarnish my name!"

Phillip hung his head and responded with a hint of devotion in his voice, "Yes, my Lord. I won't let that scum get to me again." Hand to his breast, Phillip bowed before motioning to his remaining guards and exiting the room.

"Now we are alone Ishtar, maybe you can tell me what you found in the Miditarac Mines that has decreased the Mana density so? I had big plans for that Mine." Lord Doorakian asked.

Ishtar wanted to lie to him immediately, but something came over him that left him tongue-tied and a voice was echoing in his head.

"Answer me.... Answer me.... ANSWER ME!"

"I found.... I found...." Ishtar was trying so hard not to tell him about the Orb.

"I found...a recently evolved Arachne Queen," Ishtar finally managed to tell a half-truth to fight the compulsion.

"Hmmm, did you find anything else? Why did she not kill you? This doesn't explain what I need to know." the Lord half said to himself as he was questioning Ishtar, who had sat down in the chair before the Desk without even knowing while he was fighting the compulsion.

Not sure if he was supposed to actually answer the questions or not, now the compulsion had left him, Ishtar decided to continue with his half-truths.

"I found an item related to the Black Blood Spider Queen: Clara, who was the one to evolve. She was insanely powerful but wasn't able to create another of the Sanguis, which her minions need to become Black Blood Guardians. So I gave the item back to her and in return, she spared my life. There were very few of her brood across the mines, so I assume once she evolved she either used what was creating the higher ambient mana or took it with her when she left the mine." Ishtar tried to shift Lord Doorakian's attention to Clara and her brood instead of himself.

"I will investigate this information, Ishtar. I will have Phillip keep tabs on you until I have found out what really happened down there. I don't want you running away if you haven't told me everything." the Lord replied as he was pacing the room. He then rang a small bell next to his desk before turning back to Ishtar.

"The servant will show you out Ishtar. I hope this is the last time we need to have a talk like this."

Just then Ishtar heard the door open behind him, so he stood up and walked out. Just as he got to the door, Ishtar heard the Lord muttering to himself.

"I was sure the Temple was under there. I want them all!"

*

Ishtar followed the servant in front of him with half of a mind, as he was freaking out,

"*Oh god, oh god, oh god! I need to get out of the City, he knows about the Orbs. He's going to send out troops to track and attack Clara...once that happens he will find out I was lying, I wish I had a way to warn her. She was nice enough to keep her end of the bargain, plus the longer it takes them to find her the less chance my character will get tortured before I can escape the city.*" Ishtar vigorously thought to himself.

Before he knew it, Ishtar was exiting the Castle through the main door. He couldn't even

241

remember the route he took let alone what the inside actually looked like. He went through the Main Gate only to see a couple of the Lord's Guards who had dragged him out the Leaping Fool smirking at him as if they had already been told to keep an eye on him.

Thinking of his night made him remember he wanted to go talk to Captain Kieras. Considering it hadn't been that long since he left, he should go back to see if the Gate Guards were still there.

*

Ishtar entered the tavern to find all the Gate Guards he was with earlier had left except for Captain Kieras who was sitting up at the bar looking upset. Snow was still asleep under the table where he had left her. Ishtar woke up Snow before walking over to the Captain and quietly speaking with him.

"Captain, are you ok?"

Kieras started and jumped slightly before looking over at Ishtar.

"Oh, thank god you're okay lad. I was worried when you got taken by them." he then paused before looking around quickly and then motioning Ishtar out the door, "the walls have ears lad, let's go back to my office at the Barracks."

Ishtar followed him out the door and down towards the South Gate. They passed lots of closed shops since it was late at night, before passing the fountain where Ishtar had originally spawned in what felt like forever ago. He was probably getting way too emotionally invested in the game, but he truly cared for Snow, and it seemed like Captain Kieras thought highly of him too.

Entering the barracks right behind Captain Kieras, Ishtar saw a small common room that was currently full of the Guards who had been at the tavern with him. They all jumped up out of their seats when they saw Ishtar with the Captain.

"He's back."

"He's still alive."

"Did the Captain save him?"

Ishtar heard different things as they clustered around him and Captain Kieras that had him glad he had survived and surprised that the City was still run properly if these kinds of rumours were made about Lord Doorakian. He wasn't surprised considering how the Lord looked, acted, and the fact he'd used compulsion on Ishtar.

"Settle down, you know I won't hear those malicious rumours about the Lord we follow in my barracks. You're all drunk so go to bed. Ishtar, please follow me." Captain Kieras stated.

Going up the stairs at the back of the room, Ishtar saw through the first door on his right as he followed the Captain. Through that door was one of the barracks where there were fifteen beds spread across the room, Ishtar assumed there was a squad per room. Then the first door on the left was the door Captain Kieras opened and walked through, closely followed by Ishtar.

Rather than walk completely into the room, Captain Kieras let Ishtar pass him before closing and locking the door. After he latched the door, Kieras touched an inconspicuous, ever-so-lightly coloured panel behind the door where a small rune shone for a moment. Ishtar felt a wave of magic move through the walls before it emanated into the room with his Mana Sense. As it passed a small ornament on the desk - that was the only piece of furniture in the room - a small pop was heard, and smoke rose from it. Ishtar looked at the Captain while moving to the seat in front of the desk.

Before answering Ishtar's unasked question Captain Kieras moved behind his desk and sat down before dropping his head into his hands, he then started talking without looking at Ishtar.

"I suppose you have a lot of questions about everything that happened tonight. Well, ask away before I get you out of this city. You must understand you can never come back now you have come to his attention.”

“What?” Ishtar immediately replied without actually asking any of the questions he had been thinking of this whole walk there.

“Lord Doorakian is an evil man, we believe he has been searching for something for many years using his most devoted minion Phillip. He was a childhood friend of mine before his love of power over others led him into the Lord’s service. Both the Lord and he have been implicated in necromantic rituals that have been banned in this Kingdom for a long time. There has never been enough proof for the King to act.” Captain Kieras answered.

Ishtar, wanting to help Captain Kieras but not wanting to reveal that he had one of the Orbs decided to confide in the man in front of him who said he would help him.

“Okay since I am way too low a level to combat the Lord or Phillip...hell any of the Lord’s Guards, I will agree to leave if you can get me out of the city in a few days’ time. But I do really want to know more about what’s going on? Oh, and I heard Lord Doorakian mention something about Orbs.” Ishtar responded.

"The Orbs of sealing? They have been lost since time immemorial, they are said to be a powerful elemental Orb that was used to seal away a great evil." Kieras answered slightly hesitantly as if remembering the information from long ago.

"He used compulsion on me, I told him about the Spider Queen who let me go. She was the one that evolved into an Arachne that was in the Miditaric Mines, she showed me mercy after I killed a lot of her children, so I really don't want his men to torture and kill her for information." Ishtar kept complaining about Lord Doorakian.

"Though unfortunate, he does have the right to use a spell like that on you as a Lord of the Kingdom." Kieras hedged.

"I am really quite worried about it all Captain. Side note, what was destroyed on your desk?" Ishtar replied.

"Ahh that, there is someone in my Gate Guards who has been sent to spy on me through the use of listening spells that keep appearing in my home and office. The panel on the wall activates a ward that destroys such spells." Kieras responded.

"What am I going to do Captain?" Ishtar almost begged.

"I think that's enough for tonight, you should disappear as you travellers are prone to do, I will have a room set aside for you the next couple days before helping you leave River City," Captain Kieras finished.

"Thank You for this, I will go back to my world for a time. When I return, I need to pick up some armour that Coal was making me before I leave the City," Ishtar responded.

Ishtar stood up and followed the Captain further down the hall to another set of stairs upwards, on the next floor up were a few private rooms that Ishtar assumed were for Officers. Captain Kieras led Ishtar into one of these before bidding him a good night.

Ishtar sat down on the bed for a few minutes contemplating what had happened over the last few weeks in the game. He had only accumulated about three weeks game time while at school but so much had happened to him that was drawing him into this game, like it truly was another world. He sighed to himself before logging out.

Chapter 19

Jasper was still shaken when he logged off and sat up in his bed, he took off the headset and looked at the time on the alarm clock he had on his side table.

"Hmm 5am, I guess I could try to go back to sleep for a few hours before I have to go to school...worth a shot," Jasper said to himself.

As soon as Jasper closed his eyes, he felt like he was sitting in the study with Lord Doorakian again, that suffocating presence of Death. Immediately sitting back up sweating, he felt like the game shouldn't be affecting him like it was. That Lord was terrifying, he wasn't physically imposing but all his personal guards and his Death like Aura made him feel truly dangerous in a way nothing else had in the game so far. He didn't want to try and face him in a fight till he was much more powerful. Hopefully, Captain Kieras could get Ishtar out of River City.

After a time of reflecting on his last session playing Ariair Online, Jasper moved over to his computer and continued with some homework he had. There wasn't long left in the School year, so then he could spend more time playing. Fortunately for him he only had two Final Exams that for some reason were held a few weeks before, so in class time was just to finish the various assignments he had.

Jasper only had a single assignment left to finish. So he would be spending most of his time at School that day goofing off with his friends and all of them catching up on what the others were up to in the game.

By the time it was actually time to get up and get ready for School Jasper had already finished the assignment he was going to be doing in class. His speed and quality of work had been slowly increasing over the past month he was playing the game, almost like the time compression was making his mind work more efficiently or faster outside the game or something. He submitted the work online and went to have a shower.

Upon getting out, Jasper went back to his room and got dressed for the day. As he went to leave the room without thought, he said, "C'mon Snow, time to start the day."

As soon as the words left his mouth, Ishtar froze and looked around as if only just remembering Snow wasn't there. Snow had become such an important part of his virtual life he forgot she wasn't real.

*

His first class of the day was Calculus, but because the Exam had already been taken, their teacher showed up and sat at the front of the class writing something on his laptop while leaving the students to their own devices. Unfortunately, this wasn't one of the classes he shared with Karl and Jono, so he spent his time half listening to the conversations around him while playing with his phone. One particular conversation caught his attention.

"Jess, it's been weeks why are you still so caught up on this?" It was one of the girls he didn't really know, and she was talking to her friend.

"Because! Alyse, she was the cutest little wolf that some rude guy had as a pet. I want a pet like her. Like she must have been a variant since there are only Night Wolves around River City; even though I have levelled up enough to be in the Capital now." Jess responded.

Jasper was wondering whether this girl was talking about Snow. He vaguely remembered a cute Catfolk Priest that ran up to him when he was getting back to town when he first found Snow after helping defeat the Rodent King.

Jessica had been in a few of his classes over the years, though they had never really interacted. She was a short, skinny blonde girl with a pretty face, a sharp nose, and a cheeky smile. While the girls were talking Jasper saw a small sci-fi related tattoo behind her ear as she flicked her hair.

"Jess you know I know nothing about the game. I don't play it, all I know is what you tell me." Alyse answered.

"Yeah, yeah I know. I just wish I could find them." Jess wistfully responded.

Jasper was wondering if he should ask her if she was the Catfolk from that day, but he tended to be bad at conversation a lot of the time in person, so he spent the rest of class focusing back on his phone.

*

The end of class came fast while Jasper had been absorbed reading the forums for Ariair Online. Apparently quite a few players had gotten over level fifty and were on the Lost Continent, they were spread across the four Cardinal Cities. They were finding that the monsters were incredibly strong as soon as you moved more than a day out from the cities. Fortunately for them, there were a lot of single-instance Dungeons around the cities. The lore said something about how the Lost Continent had a higher mana density than the four starter Kingdoms so had a much higher chance of spawning a Dungeon.

That was as far as he got before the bell rang and the class ended. As he was about to walk out the door the people in front of him suddenly stopped, it would appear there was a fight between a couple of freshmen just outside their class. Before long it was broken up by teachers, they were stuck in the class for a couple more minutes until the hall cleared. As it turned out the people directly in front of him were Jess and Alyse, and seeing as they were stuck, Jasper decided to ask the question.

"Hey, Jess, right?" Jasper started.

Knowing of Jasper but not really knowing him well Jess was a bit hesitant with her answer, "Uh…. yeah, you're Jasper, aren't you?"

"Yeah, I am, I couldn't help but hear your conversation before about a variant Wolf that is a pet." Jasper answered.

Jess's awkward attitude disappeared as if it had never existed when she heard him say that.

"What? Have you seen her? Do you play Ariair Online? Where are you? What race are you playing?" she excitedly asked. Jasper was visibly taken aback by her slew of questions to such an extent that Alyse started laughing.

"Hahaha sorry dude, she is super excitable about that game. Now Jess, what have we said about breathing when we get excited?"

"Sorry guys, I just really enjoy playing and that wolf was the cutest pet I have seen in the game. Mind you she was also the only pet I've seen that didn't belong to a Beastmaster," Jess answered.

Jasper chuckled and said "I guess you could say Snow is a special case. She was the runt and only protected by the Alpha of her pack, but he died, so I took care of her for him."

"WHAT! You are the Draconian who walked away from me when all I wanted to do was pet her?!" Jess exclaimed.

A little scared of the angry girl even though she was half his size Jasper made placating gestures and tried to explain.

"I'm sorry, I had just found her after a really difficult dungeon that left me exhausted. First being attacked by her pack then helping them to kill a Unique Boss Mob."

Jess half glared at him before huffing. "What's your game name? I still want to meet Snow, so I will add you and then we can meet up."

"…….ok…. it's Ishtar. I was planning on going to Cindera next anyway." Jasper hesitantly answered before seeing the hallway was clear now so walked off to his next class which was Gym with a hurried "Bye" as he left.

*

Jasper was planning on talking to Jono and Karl during class, but the Gym Teacher kept the boys huffing and sweating the whole time. It wasn't until they sat down at lunch they could actually start talking about everything.

"Hey guys," Jasper said as he finally sat down at the table with Jono and Karl, "so what level and where are you guys now?"

"What took you so long? Anyway, I'm level thirty-five now and doing quests for the King so I won't have to pay my way to the Lost Continent when I hit level fifty." Jono said. "Also teamed up with some guys to run a dungeon a few times."

"Sounds good, pretty standard. Would have thought you would be skulking through all sorts of underground places with your class?" Jasper asked.

"Nah the King's army has taken control of the whole country since some crazy Naga chick drowned most of a town and stole a boat before destroying the rest that were at the docks. No one

254

knows where she went, but there is a crazy big bounty on her head that I wish I could get. Even the Adventurer's Guild has been taken over, it's crazy. It's why I'm working crazy hard for them to try and get an exemption to leave the country before level fifty." Jono answered.

"This game sure is living up to the hype, it really does feel like a real world, even most of the Dungeons disappear after someone completes them a single time. Apparently, they have found one of the resetting dungeons on the Lost Continent though." Karl responded.

"By the way I got you beat though, I'm already level fifty-three because of the Quests I was given by the Red Rose Assassins Guild. It's affiliated with one of the secret crime syndicates. I was taught poisons and got an insane amount of Exp and a couple titles for assassinating a few guys over fifty Levels above me, though I am still indebted to the Guild for hundreds of gold." Karl chimed in.

"Oh cool, what is the title and what does it do?" Ishtar asked

"Prodigy Assassin. It gives me a 250% Damage bonus to backstab on anything more than twenty-five levels above me." Karl answered.

"Wow yeah, that would make levelling easy considering the more levels above you the enemy is, the more EXP you get, with some good buffs you can probably one-shot some enemies." Jono chimed in.

"Yeah man, I hooked up with this group of super strong dudes too. I'm not allowed to join their Guild but their Leader, who goes by Justice, essentially hired me as a freelance fighter when he found out about my title." Karl continued.

"Cool man, hey don't get too far ahead of us though. How are we supposed to play together when we are all in there otherwise?" Jasper said.

"Don't worry man, I got this...hey wait! You haven't told us how you are doing." Karl responded.

Jasper knew he was much weaker in levels, though with his titles and all the training he has done, he may very well be as strong as Jono. Due to this he decided to half lie and told them he was at a higher level than he was but only tell them about one of his titles.

"Haha sorry almost forgot, I'm level twenty-five and have a pretty awesome title. It's called Seeker of the Hidden that actually ranks up when I find new unique things." Jasper said.

"Dude that is pretty cool, what does the title do?" Jono asked.

"It gives me plus one to every stat per level and it's currently level three," Jasper answered.

Karl's mouth dropped open at what Jasper had just told him, in an incredulous voice he asked Jasper "You have a Title that gives you an extra twenty-four stat points?! That's over three levels worth of stats."

"Yeah, a little closer to five bud...um, just think, as a group, we are even more powerful?" Jasper said with a grin, pleased that he didn't tell them all the perks of his other title as they probably would have lost their minds.

That was when lunch finished, and the three had to part ways again. Just as they went to separate Jasper realised they hadn't added each other to their friend's list in the game yet.

"Meh, next time," he thought to himself.

*

Jasper walked out of another lesson at the Dojo feeling better than he had all day. He was the fittest he had been in years, he really felt getting the correct form and stance at the Dojo was helping him fight in-game. He just had to change everything ever so slightly to accommodate the different body shape.

He thought he was almost good enough to move up to the Intermediate class soon.

*

Glen stood watching his class leave while his Assistant Instructor was packing everything up, he was especially focused on Jasper. The boy had been progressing at an abnormally fast pace though he did have a tendency to swing his Bokken oddly at times, Glen had no option but to assume he was constantly practising everything he was taught in Ariair Online with its time compression, so getting that much more practice than anyone else. Glen wondered if Jasper had noticed how much weight he had lost and how much muscle he had put on with how the headsets work, or didn't work properly.

Glen turned to his Assistant, "Pete, go home. I will finish up, thank you for your help tonight" he said with a slight bow.

"Ok, goodbye Sensei" Pete bowed and left.

It didn't take Glen very long to finish packing everything up and sweep the floor. Once he had finished, he locked the dojo and turned the lights off. He then moved to the door in his office, that no one ever really noticed, and up to his apartment.

It was time for him to become a Human Monk again.

*

In a dark office, a woman sat behind a large desk with a built-in touchscreen computer. A man in an expensive suit stood on the other side of the desk looking uncomfortable. She ignored him and kept using her computer for another few minutes.

Finally, she looked up at him.

"Director Stevenson, why have you been interfering with Ariair?" she asked.

"I have no idea what you mean Madam CEO. I put quite a bit of time and money to get this project off the ground, it's why I'm on the board. Why would I want to interfere with the game?" he smoothly answered.

"I'm talking about how you used some of the programmers to find high-level equipment in the Human Kingdom to gift your idiot son!" she accused.

"So I gave him a little help. It's not like I gave him anything Legendary level, it was just an Epic set of armour. He will out-level it by level 100 anyway." Stevenson responded.

The woman glared at him for a moment before sighing and finally answering, "Don't interfere with my game again. He will sink or swim on his own from now on.”

“Fine, but he will be the Hero of his own story. He needs the experience ruling and making the right decisions to one day take over my position.” Stevenson answered.

“Whatever, get out of my office now.” the CEO finished in a tired voice.

Director Stevenson almost made it to the door before his phone rang, the CEO saw him look at the caller ID before answering it, “What did he do this time?” was the last thing she heard as the door closed behind him.

She looked back at her computer screen, on it appeared images that shouldn’t exist. Four different individuals were each in different places and doing different things. Looking at one particular image, she spoke out loud to herself.

“I’m still not sure why I gave you that title. I guess I liked you the best of the four, I hope it’s you who collects the orbs.”

Chapter 20 – Around Town

Ishtar logged back into the room that Captain Kieras had set aside for him the morning of the day his armour should have been ready. He didn't want to go see Coal too quickly just in case one of the Lord's men was watching either him or Coal. Just because Captain Kieras's men seemed loyal to him didn't mean none of them were informing the Lord of what was going on in the Barracks. Ishtar hadn't checked his status page for a while, so he decided to give it a look.

Status
Name: *Ishtar*
Alignment: *Good*
Level: *15*   **Exp:** *21666/25000*
Class: *Elemental Knight*
Race: *Elemental Draconian*
Money: *33G 45S 75C* **Gender:** *Male*
Title: *Seeker of the Hidden III*
Chosen of Thia
Fame: *460*   **Infamy:** *0*
-

Health: *580/580*   **Health Regen:** *5.3/Sec*
Mana: *780/780*   **Mana Regen:** *31.0/Sec*
Stamina: *450/450*   **Stamina Regen:** *7.0/Sec*

-

Strength: *65 (85)*   **Dexterity:** *25 (31)*
Agility: *27 (33)*   **Endurance:** *38 (45)*
Vitality: *45 (53)*   **Intelligence:** *56 (78)*

Wisdom: *23 (29)*   **Luck:** *12 (16)*
Free Stat Points: *8*

-

Affinity:
Water: 100%
Air: 100%
Earth: 100%
Light: 100%
Lightning: 100%
Ice: 100%
Arcane: 100%
Fire:100%

-

Orbs
Fire

He had certainly grown more powerful even though his level hadn't changed by that much, mostly due to his two titles which gave him a fantastic boost of power. His gains from his change of Race wouldn't really kick in till he gained a few more levels.

Ishtar left Snow in the room given to him by Captain Kieras while considering how to spend his time that day since he was trapped in the City. It wasn't worth the risk of trying to leave until Captain Kieras was ready to smuggle him away from those observing him. As Ishtar was thinking about that he was moving through the Barracks until he spotted one of the Guards he actually remembered from the tavern. Since he was alone in the common area eating Ishtar decided to approach him.

"Hey, sorry I don't remember your name, but do you know where the Captain is?" Ishtar asked.

The Guard looked up at him before smiling and responding, "The name's Bull, well that's what everyone calls me. I'm pretty sure he is at the North Gate today, he is in the middle of organising the monthly Patrol that goes from here to the Capital."

"Thanks, Bull. By the way, thanks for being welcoming with me at the Tavern the other night" Ishtar responded as he turned to leave.

"No worries buddy, we had fun till shit hit the fan haha" Bull answered as Ishtar was leaving.

Ishtar figured that was how the Captain was getting him out of the City so decided to go to the Adventurer's Guild to check what quests were available. As Ishtar was walking through the City, he was fairly certain people were watching him, but that could have just been his fear of Lord Doorakian.

It wasn't until he was near to the Adventurer's Guild that he happened to look up at the roof of a nearby building, glimpsing a figure dressed in black watching him. The shape jerked backwards to avoid being seen as Ishtar looked upwards. Slightly pleased that he didn't actually imagine things, Ishtar went into the Guildhall.

He walked up to the reception desk first. There was a small line of people handing in quests so while he was waiting, Ishtar looked around the room. On the other side where there were tables and the bar, Ishtar noticed there were a few individuals that looked lost or had amazed looks on their faces. He figured out these were newer players. He surmised that there must have been another batch of the headsets released.

Everyone who started within the first couple of weeks had already grown in Levels and left for the other areas of the County. He was an exception to that rule given how long it took him to do the Hidden Dungeon, find the Temple and his hellish week with Quattra. He felt he wouldn't have gotten so deeply ingrained in Ariair if it wasn't for meeting Snow in the Realm of the Rodent King or meeting and hearing of the betrayal of Thia. He truly wasn't certain if everything was deeply affecting him more than it should. His friends still treated it like it was merely fun without any consequences, yet Ishtar felt like his actions had a real effect on the world around him.

Trying to shake his dark thoughts Ishtar focused back on the line just as the last person between him and the reception desk finished, and it was his turn.

"Hi, I just had an enquiry about when completing Quests." Ishtar started.

The male Snakefolk on the other side of the desk looked bored and just responded with a nod and a grunt.

"Do I have to return to the same branch to finish any Quests I take there, or can I finish them anywhere as long as I have the proof?" Ishtar asked.

The Snakefolk smothered a tsk, "Well that depends on the type of Quest. Escort Quests naturally get handed in at the destination, Extermination Quests can be handed in anywhere since it's normally the Government that creates them. Finally, Investigation Quests depend on wherever the commissioner is. Since Quests are shared between the Guildhalls depending on where the Quest area is, you normally need to return to where it was commissioned as opposed to where you started it. This is why we register any Quests taken to your Guild Card." the receptionist concisely explained.

Ishtar thanked him and walked over to the Quest Board. Since he was now a D rank, there were more missions available for him. Given that Captain Kieras was going to be headed to the Capital, Ishtar decided getting Quests that led him in that direction would be for the best. He found a Goblin Extermination and a Direwolf culling that were both in the forests just south of Cindera. These were fairly standard Quests in most games, so he figured they were good options to increase his level and standing in the Guild once he escaped the city. He took the chits off the board and took them back to the Receptionist to register them to his card.

Now that Ishtar had finished at the Adventurer's Guild he chose to go to the Mage Guild to pay to upgrade a few of his abilities to the Intermediate level. It took very little time to walk there and upgrade his Appraisal, Meditation and Stone Skin.

Skill Upgraded:
Appraisal Beginner Level 9 >> Appraisal Basic Level 1
More information can now be seen about higher level items, Monsters and Beasts.

Skill Upgraded:
Meditation Beginner Level 9 >> Meditation Basic Level 1
The user is still aware of their surroundings even while meditation is in effect.

Ability Upgraded:
Stone Skin Beginner Level 9 >> Metal Coat Basic Level 1
Turn your skin into a harder substance to increase your defence.
Natural Defence +100%
Speed -20% due to extreme weight

Unfortunately, Metal Coat was a double-edged shield, but Ishtar was assured that the Speed restriction would be reduced as it increased in level, and when the Ability was upgraded to Master it would disappear completely. Plus, due to his good standing with the Mage Guild, the upgrades only cost 1G each even though it was a different worker than the last time he had been there.

Just as Ishtar was about to leave he had a thought, turning back to the Store Clerk he asked,

"By any chance do you know how I can get around constantly having to let my Pet get the Kill and full experience from our Kills? Sharing experience would be much easier."

"Why didn't you just make your pet your familiar? Only Beastmasters' can share their experience with pets." the Clerk answered in an incredulous tone.

"Ummm because I didn't even know that was possible let alone how to do it?" Ishtar answered.

"Haha well, I have a book here on that for the low low price of 5G out of my personal library." the Clerk responded going straight into salesman mode.

"Fine," Ishtar answered as he grabbed the book out of the Clerk's hand who had a massive grin on his face. This time Ishtar left and headed back towards the barracks.

As he walked Ishtar read the short book that he had just bought only to find out he had been fleeced. The book was handwritten, most of it was advice on finding a familiar. Only the last page went over the way to share Mana with the Beast to set up the Familiar relationship. That would be almost exactly the same as his unique pet bond except for the ability to share Experience.

Not sure if his Armour would be finished by Coal yet Ishtar decided to go back to the Barracks to make Snow his familiar before going to visit Coal to get his new Armour.

Ishtar walked back into his current room finding Snow had been asleep the whole time he was gone, he thought it was probably a good thing since she hadn't been sleeping much while he was around. He felt a little bad about waking Snow since she looked so peaceful. Ishtar relaxed in a chair near the bed and watched Snow for a bit.

It wasn't even half an hour later as Ishtar was starting to slip into a nap that Snow woke up and snapped him out of his stupor.

"Master why are you sitting there watching me?" she asked.

"I was coming to change you from a pet to my Familiar, we will have a deeper connection though we both might be changed a bit from mixing of our mana. Would you like to do it?" Ishtar explained then asked.

"I trust you, Master. You have taken care of me since we met." Snow answered.

"Ok, this shouldn't hurt a bit. All we need to do is be touching and then send a little bit of our Mana into the other's core which will form a connection," Ishtar explained, secretly hoping he read the book right.

Ishtar moved to the floor next to Snow and sat cross-legged on the ground next to her in a meditative pose and placed his hand on her nape, initially petting her before concentrating on slowly moving his mana down his arm to her body. He felt a barrier at her skin preventing his mana from entering her.

"Snow I need you to let my mana in," Ishtar asked.

Almost as soon as he asked her, Ishtar felt the barrier disappear from Snow. Once his mana was in her body, he couldn't figure out where his mana was supposed to go to start the connection. He noticed all her mana seemed to be flowing from a spot near her heart, tracing it back to where it was coming from Ishtar was shocked to find out Snow had a Mana Core. He had read only high-class monsters had mana cores, no monsters in the starting countries should have them, though it did mean that since she was a variant, she could become incredibly powerful.

As soon as his mana touched her core, her mana responded by flickering all the different elemental colours to his senses before releasing a pure Light mana string back along the mana he had injected into her, following it all the way back to his chest in into his centre. Ishtar felt a slight twinge as this happened but that was all, a screen popped up in front of him shortly after.

You have performed the ritual to make the Light Wolf (variant) 'Snow' your familiar.
You now share 50% of all Exp from kills regardless of contribution to damage
You can now sense each other's location through your mana connection
Congratulations on your new bond!

"Master I'm sleepy again." was the only response from Snow upon the completion of the bond.

"Ok little one, go have a nap. I will go see Coal to get my new armour" Ishtar responded, knowing he couldn't keep calling her 'little one' as her head was up to his mid-thigh now. She was growing as she levelled.

"Hehe, I will probably be able to ride her by the time she's level fifty at the speed she is growing," Ishtar thought to himself with a laugh.

Fortunately for Ishtar, staying at the Guards Barracks meant Coal's workshop was just down the stairs and around the corner.

For the first time when Ishtar walked into Coal's workshop, Coal wasn't in the main area working; someone else was there making horseshoes. Ishtar assumed that meant this younger looking Bearfolk was Coal's apprentice, he finished what he was making before Ishtar asked,

"Hey, I'm looking for Coal. My name is Ishtar, he told me to come back around now."

"Ishtar," the apprentice repeated, "he said you were coming sooner or later. Out the back in his private area, just walk through the doors." was the reply.

Ishtar followed the instructions finding a short hallway through the doorway, there were two doors one on each side of the hallway. Ishtar tried the one on the left to find a storeroom completely full of Iron, Steel and better Armour and Weapons of all types. Not seeing Coal in the main room Ishtar tried the other door, which was also locked. The only thing for Ishtar to do was knock.

KNOCK *KNOCK*

Instead of the door opening, Ishtar heard movement behind the door,

"Who's there?" Coal yelled through the door.

"It's Ishtar, I'm here to collect the Armour you're making for me" Ishtar answered.

The door was wrenched open, and Coal dragged Ishtar into the room.

"Shh not too loud, why didn't you tell me the Lord had his eye on you! I had one of his pet Guards in here asking why you had come to see me! Do you have any idea what would happen if they found out I had Electrum?" Coal whispered harshly.

"I didn't know he was looking for me when I saw you last. His men came to the tavern when I was with Captain Kieras and some of the Guards took me to see the Lord. It was because I finished the quest to clear out the Miditarac Mines that they were looking for me. The Lord was looking for something, and I think he thought it was there." Ishtar tried to explain.

"Well, Ishtar you have put me in a pretty tough position now. I can't make anything or even be seen with what remains of the Electrum while I'm in River City and my contract with the Guards is for another five years. Though this armour was probably the hardest and most enjoyable project, I have ever made. It is also the best thing I have ever made, it pushed my Blacksmithing to Expert Level Eight. It took me an entire year to get it from level four to level seven, this one project with such high-quality materials got it to level eight." Coal excitedly, yet still slightly upset, added.

Knowing he was going to have to make a sacrifice for this armour Ishtar made a decision.

"I know you said you would make the armour for me and add in some Gold but since this is causing so much trouble for you why don't you forget about the Gold." Ishtar said out loud while thinking *"This armour better be worth the sacrifice I'm making for it."*

"No that's fine I just can't afford to give you nearly as much. I was going to be going into debt to pay the 250G and make it up quickly with making items using the Electrum, but since I can't do that, I will still offer you 50G for the remainder of the Electrum. Though I did fudge the records and 'borrow' some High-Grade Coal to turn your Black Blood Iron into Black Blood Steel before making an alloy from that Steel and the Electrum." Coal answered. His face then turned upward into a big grin, "So do you want to see it?" he asked.

"Of course," Ishtar answered with an equally large grin.

Coal moved out of the way and on a wooden stand behind him, sat a beautiful (in his eyes) set of armour. The Black Blood Iron had clearly been turned into steel as it was now a dark grey set of Plate armour with artistic Electrum filled designs etched into the chestplate that has the pauldrons attached and a slitted face helmet with slightly intimidating horns on top. The design was a Kite shield with a wolf that looked an awful lot like Snow lying at the bottom, the boots and gauntlets followed the theme with Electrum gilding etched into them in a swirl pattern leading all the way to small tips leading to the claws on the gauntlets.

"The electrum into the fingertips will cause increased damage from any spells that use your arms, and the enchantments on the chestplate increases durability and defence. The legs have an enchantment to lessen the weight of the whole armour down to the equivalent weight of leather armour. The tips of the gauntlets have been sharpened and can be used as weapons themselves. The helmet has a wind block so no matter how fast you are moving or the wind in the environment you will not end up blind, and finally, the boots can increase your speed. This is why the cost of enchantment was going to be so much even for me. The electrum was used as gilding throughout the whole set which is why so many enchantments can be supported."

Ishtar used his newly upgraded Appraisal on the Armour set.

Ishtar's Wolf Helmet
Type: *Helmet* **Durability:** *500/500*
Quality: *Epic* **Defence:** *75*

The Helmet in the unique set of Armour created by the Expert blacksmith for the Adventurer Ishtar. Created using metal grown by a monster and the legendary metal Electrum.
Full Set Bonus: +10 Agility

Enchantment:
Faceshield

Ishtar's Wolf Chestplate
Type: *Chestplate* **Durability:** *500/500*
Quality: *Epic* **Defence:** *200*

The Chestplate in the unique set of Armour created by the Expert blacksmith for the Adventurer Ishtar. Created using metal grown by a monster and the legendary metal Electrum.
Full Set Bonus: +10 Intelligence

Enchantments:
Increased Durability
Increased Defence

Ishtar's Wolf Gauntlets
Type: *Gauntlets* **Durability:** *500/500*
Quality: *Epic* **Defence:** *75*

The Gauntlets in the unique set of Armour created by the Expert blacksmith for the Adventurer Ishtar. Created using metal grown by a monster and the legendary metal Electrum
Attack Damage: 25-50
Full Set Bonus: +10 Strength

Enchantments:
Decreased Mana Cost
Increased Magic Damage

Ishtar's Wolf Greaves
Type: *Greaves* **Durability:** *500/500*
Quality: *Epic* **Defence:** *150*
The Greaves in the unique set of Armour created by the Expert blacksmith for the Adventurer Ishtar. Created using metal grown by a monster and the legendary metal Electrum.
Full Set Bonus: +10 Vitality
Enchantment:
Decreased Weight

Ishtar's Wolf Boots
Type: *Boots* **Durability:** *500/500*
Quality: *Epic* **Defence:** *75*
The pair of Boots in the unique set of Armour created by the Expert blacksmith for the Adventurer Ishtar. Created using metal grown by a monster and the legendary metal Electrum.
Full Set Bonus: + 10 Endurance
Enchantment:
Increased Movement Speed

"Holy Crap! That's some incredible armour. With this, I won't need to change it until I'm like level 100!" Ishtar exclaimed after seeing the stats on his new armour.

"Good to see you like it. I had to name it since it came out as an Epic set of armour. I saw how much you cared for the wolf, so that's why it's named after her. I do have some bad news though, you can't actually wear the new armour until you leave the city though. It can't get out that there is Electrum anywhere. Also, here is that 50G." Coal responded as he handed Ishtar a bag of money.

Ishtar stored the armour set in his inventory, thanked Coal and went back to the front of the barracks. As he was about to enter the door, he saw Captain Kieras arriving back.

"Ishtar its time," he said as soon as he got to Ishtar.

Chapter 21

"Ishtar it's time."

With those words, Ishtar felt like his heart was in his throat.

"Ok, what's the plan to get me away from here?" Ishtar asked tentatively.

"This is not a good place to talk about it. Follow me." Captain Kieras answered.

Kieras moved towards the door into the barracks proper and through the common room, only a single mage wearing a robe that covered their whole body with the hood up was there. Kieras nodded knowingly to them. The mage stood up and followed Kieras and Ishtar up to the room that had been set aside for Ishtar. Inside, he looked around and had to give Snow a double take. Upon seeing her, a new notification appeared for Ishtar.

Your familiar 'Snow' has evolved into a Light Direwolf (Variant)
Your unique mana has given your familiar help in taking a step further down her ancestral bloodline, the Legendary Fenrir.

Snow had grown. Her fur was still the Snow white except for on her paws; they had changed to black. Like her father's. She stretched roughly three metres in length from tip of her nose to the tip of her tail, and once she stood up, Ishtar saw that her head came up to his chest.

"Damn you got big Snow." Ishtar unnecessarily exclaimed.

"I don't know how this happened master, I went to sleep and woke up much bigger. I thought the room was shrinking so I kind of broke it." Snow tried to explain.

Ishtar hadn't even noticed the state of the room until Snow had mentioned it, the bed was in shreds, and most of the furniture had been smashed to splinters. Snow was standing in the only spot that wasn't covered in wood splinters. Ishtar wondered how good the soundproofing in this room was considering no one noticed this happening.

Captain Kieras and the mage had followed Ishtar into the room and were shocked at both the difference in Snow and the devastation of the room. It didn't take long before Captain Kieras ignored the devastation since there were more pressing matters. He looked at the mage and nodded before turning back to Ishtar and starting to talk.

"Ishtar, Snow being this big didn't factor into the plan. I have no idea how to get her out of the city being this big. I had planned on putting her in the cart we are taking with the patrol to Cindera while you dressed as one of the Guards." he explained.

"All the way to Cindera? I would have thought you only patrol near River City since you are the Gate Guards. Won't they recognise me though?" Ishtar responded with.

"Rather than using a courier to send the reports to the capital we just use the Guards to do a patrol going to Cindera then on the way back go through the side villages. This normally takes up to two weeks. My friend here, who doesn't want to give his name, will be casting an illusion on you to appear like one of my other Draconian Guards." Captain Kieras explained the plan.

"I can't leave Snow though, she was hurt because of me once, I won't leave her here." Ishtar insisted.

"Master, I uh have a new ability with my new body." Snow spoke up.

Her body then proceeded to shimmer and disappear from view with only a sense of movement when she moved quickly.

"That's an excellent camouflage ability your Wolf has. It's a high-level light magic spell for a Mage, but it's inherent in some beasts." the mage spoke for the first time in a surprisingly deep voice.

"She should be able to keep it up for around an hour considering her size and the strength I feel from her." he continued.

"We leave in half an hour at the North Gate. Put on this armour and these weapons and only come out when no one else is in the hallway. The guard you will be impersonating is one of my agents, so he is staying at a safe house with enough food for a week, so no one notices he is still here until you are long gone." Captain Kieras left as soon as he finished speaking.

Now alone with the Mage, Ishtar just stood there looking at him since he was unsure of what to say. The Mage didn't want to get involved himself so just started chanting and crafting the illusion. Ten minutes later Ishtar formed a mirror with water mana to see he was looking slimmer and also a deep shade of Green with a touch of blue across the top of his wings. It wasn't until he got rid of the mirror and looked at the Mage did he see the tension in the man's demeanour.

"I've always been jealous of the ability of Draconians to be so natural with their element like that. No chanting or forming of spells, you can just manipulate it at will…. My illusion will last around four hours which will get you out of the City." the Mage said through gritted teeth before then leaving the room.

Ishtar found himself alone in the room with Snow and only twenty minutes before he had to be at the North Gate to meet the rest of the caravan. He looked at the Armour but didn't bother using Appraisal since he wouldn't be wearing it for long enough for it to matter. He did pay more attention to the Sword and Shield he was given though.

River City Iron Broadsword
Type: *Broadsword* ***Durability:*** *50/50*
Quality: *Common* ***Damage:*** *15-25*
The standard sword mass produced for all Guards in River City by the contracted Blacksmith Coal

River City Kite Shield
Type: *Shield* ***Durability:*** *50/50*
Quality: *Common* ***Defence:*** *45 (145) when using Guard*
The Shield made for Sergeant's in the River City Gate Guards by the contracted Blacksmith Coal

The sword could never be sold since it was literally made for the Guards, but the Shield was great until he could buy a better one. Although his sword was better than this one it was too distinctive to keep on him. Storing his current armour that he would soon need to sell as scrap metal and his sword Ishtar equipped the Leather greaves and padded leather top, overlaid with an Iron Cuirass and vambraces. On top of all this was a tabard bearing the City's Coat of Arms, a Shield with crossed swords being held up by a pair of Dragons.

Finished getting ready Ishtar prepared himself to leave the City and potentially never come back.

"Snow it's time to go. Use your camouflage before you leave the room and then slowly make your way to the North Gate and into the Forest. Track us but don't come to us until we stop the first night, so we are far enough away from town" Ishtar ordered Snow

"Yes, Master. Please be safe. Goodbye." With those parting words, Snow became invisible and after opening the door all Ishtar could hear was her nails clicking on the wooden floor as she left.

*

Ishtar arrived at the North Gate to find a group of a half-dozen Gate Guards finishing loading up a pair of carts with Captain Kieras standing to the side supervising. Ishtar walked over to him since he didn't want anything to seem out of place and he had no idea what to do.

"Captain." Ishtar greeted.

"Don't talk, your voice doesn't sound right. I need you to sit next to me on the first cart. This is where the Sergeant sits anyway. The squad will do their work without any input since they all know what's going on. You may recognise them." Captain Kieras quietly responded.

Ishtar made a point of looking around to see just who the Guards were, it turned out all of them were part of the group from the Tavern. These men were going out of their way to help get Ishtar out of the City. Ishtar was unsure if it was from loyalty to Captain Kieras or due to them actually liking Ishtar and wanting to help him. Either way, Ishtar was touched that they would defy Lord Doorakian.

It was less than twenty minutes later when they were ready to go, so Ishtar followed Captain Kieras over to the lead cart and sat down on the driver's bench next to him. The Captain picked up the reins and flicked them to get the horses moving as he yelled.

"Let's move out."

*

Phillip stepped up to and bowed before Lord Doorakian's desk.

"My Lord, we found the Arachne," he stated.

"And?" Lord Doorakian intoned.

"No matter how we tortured her and her filthy spawn in front of her she refused to talk, so we killed her. No treasure that was important was found in her nest, so I gave it to the men to further secure

284

their loyalty. They believe I did it against your wishes." Phillip continued.

"DAMMIT! That bastard managed to lie to me! Go to the people we have trailing him and bring him to me." Lord Doorakian demanded.

"I will get the seekers report at once," Phillip asked.

"Good, now go." Lord Doorakian demanded.

*

Phillip slammed the door to Lord Doorakian's office open as he scrambled into the room.

"My Lord they have lost him! Kieras took him to the barracks, and they haven't seen him since. One of my agents in the Gate Guards says he left with his pet." he explained.

"Use the hounds and take some of my forces to track them down and kill them all for defying me. I ordered that Adventurer confined to the City and I expect my orders to be followed!" Lord Doorakian ordered Phillip.

*

It was late afternoon when the Guards stopped to make camp. Once again Ishtar didn't know how to help, so he stood off to the side with Captain Kieras who had already removed a tent from his inventory and was well into setting it up.

"Ishtar, now you look like yourself again. You can speak. It was only in the City where there were eyes on the lookout for you that that was an issue." Captain Kieras stated when he saw Ishtar walking towards him.

"I will be back in a few minutes, Snow has been shadowing us all day and I want to go get her, so none of your Guards freak out," Ishtar replied before walking towards the trees.

Ishtar was starting to feel tired even though he hadn't really done anything that day; just quietly rode on the cart next to the Captain. He vaguely knew where Snow was with their new closer bond, so he walked straight towards where he felt her.

She must have been training her camouflage all day since he knew she was near, but it wasn't until Ishtar was nudged from behind that she stopped using it and playfully jumped on him.

"Hey, I missed you today. Just wish I could talk to you mentally like you can to me." Ishtar said.

"But you do Master, I hear you with my mind as well as my ears. Try saying something directed at me." Snow answered with a chuckle.

"Can you hear me, Snow?" Ishtar tried to send to Snow mentally.

"Of course," Snow immediately replied.

You have discovered one of the secrets of the Familiar Bond!
You can now communicate with your Familiar mentally without a mana cost.
There are still more secrets to uncover as your bond grows stronger. Can you discover them?

Ishtar was slightly annoyed that he never realised and was impressed with the ability to actually mentally communicate with Snow. He knew they would have to test it to see the distance, but it would make hunting with her more efficient when he didn't have to yell out the strategy.

As they were walking back to the camp Ishtar was practising speaking mentally to Snow without actually moving his mouth or even looking at her, being able to have the conversation without anyone else knowing may help them in the future.

Ishtar was reminded why he went to fetch Snow himself once he returned to the camp. Even these men who had met her before only saw her as a monster. At least two of them yelled for an attack and started to draw their weapons before a commanding voice rang out.

"BELAY THAT! That is Ishtar's pet Snow, she has just evolved." Captain Kieras bellowed.

The men started to settle down and move back towards the fire in the middle of five tents. Apparently, they had brought and put up a tent for Ishtar as well. Hanging above the fire was a cooking pot that was starting to smell good.

Within twenty minutes the seven of the group of eight were all sated and relaxing while one was on sentry duty, though Ishtar knew they needn't bother with Snow around, she would alert them if anything came near.

Twilight was just hinting when Ishtar felt alertness coming from Snow.

"*Danger, I smell death,*" She told him.

"Something is coming!" Ishtar yelled to the others as he equipped his new armour and his better sword.

Chapter 22 - Ambush

"Danger, I smell death"

"Something is coming!"

Ishtar immediately felt stronger with the added stats from his new armour. He got ready for whatever Snow had noticed. She had started prowling near Ishtar facing towards the woods, looking from side to side like she couldn't pin down where the scent was coming from.

"Snow, where are they coming from?" Ishtar asked.

"I can't tell, the scent of death is everywhere" she responded.

A demonic howl came from Ishtar's left.

HOWL

Ishtar turned to check on the others, they had moved to the side of the fire so that they could benefit from the light but were not too close to falling into it during combat.

Ishtar began to head to where they were when another howl came from the other side of the group, which caused them all to turn their heads towards the noise. As soon as they looked in that direction, a shadow leapt from behind one of the tents, straight towards one of the Guards. As the shadow got closer to the fire, its appearance came into focus, it was a decaying wolf with solid red glowing eyes. Ishtar wasn't sure what the hell it was, but it looked like a zombie or demon wolf. Quickly using Appraisal since he knew Snow would protect him.

Zombie Hound
Type: *Undead* ***Level:*** *20*
Health: *200*
A canine that has been reanimated by some form of
necromantic magic

In shock, everyone except Captain Kieras froze as the Hound ripped out the throat of the Guard. He kicked the hound off the guard's body but didn't have any healing items so just looked at the man on the ground in despair.

Ishtar, on the other hand, tried using his Minor Heal which healed the guard for 100HP but did nothing to stop the massive blood loss, unfortunately, he would need to upgrade it before it could close such a serious wound and replace the blood loss. The situation just proved that no matter how strong you were, if you didn't defend against a vital attack from a similar level enemy, you can die easily. The hound was only five levels above Ishtar, so he figured he could take it with the buffs from his armour.

Ishtar tried casting Minor Heal on the Hound since traditionally Healing spells damaged undead monsters. It worked doing 100 damage while Captain Kieras's kick had already done around 75 damage, so a single Cleave from Ishtar took its head clean off.

As Ishtar had been moving to kill the first Hound that appeared, the other guards had circled up with their shields facing out and had been attacked by another Hound that collectively the remaining five guards had hacked to pieces in seconds. Behind him, Ishtar heard Snow growl and leap. After finishing off the first one, he turned around to find Snow with her jaws around a third Hound's neck, while her claws glowed brightly from expelling her Light Claws spell.

"Ishtar you have a Healing spell?" Captain Kieras asked while this was all happening.

"Yeah but it's only Minor Heal so it won't save his life, his wound is too severe and the bleeding too heavy. I'm sorry." Ishtar replied as he and Snow moved to stand at ready with the Captain.

"Gods be Damned! This must be the doing of Lord Doorakian! He and his abominations." Captain Kieras cursed.

"Haha well give the man a prize!" a voice rang out from the woods. A voice that Ishtar knew, Phillip stepped into view surrounded by another dozen

Zombie Hounds as well as a half dozen Zombie Guards.

Ishtar was so shocked at the sight that he forgot to use Appraisal on the new Zombies, he recognised these faces too. These were the some of the Lord's Guards that had been with Phillip when they took Ishtar to the Lord.

"Phillip, how far you have fallen to be a part of this," Captain Kieras uttered as he prepared his weapon, eyes only for Phillip. "Men, work together to defend yourself. I will kill Phillip. Ishtar, you and your wolf take the hounds."

"Yes, Sir!" was the response from the remains of the squad.

"Kill the Guards and the Wolf, the master wants the Adventurer," Phillip ordered as he advanced towards Captain Kieras.

The Zombie Guards and half the Zombie Hounds advanced at the circled Guards while the remaining Hounds came at Ishtar and Snow.

Ishtar activated Metal Coat to increase his defence before raising his Shield and spamming Minor Heal four times to kill the closest two Hounds. That was all he could afford to use since it was a mana intensive spell. The largest Hound by far that looked like it was once the leader of the pack attacked

Snow with one of the lesser while the remaining two ran at Ishtar. Ishtar took one last look around at the beginning of the melee before he had to focus on the Hounds attacking him.

With the increasing lack of light in the area other than the fire, Ishtar placed the fire at his back while activating his Fire Eyes causing his eyes to glow as the area became as bright as day. A sentient enemy might be intimidated by this ability, but the simple mind of the Zombie Hound's didn't even stutter instep. One leapt at Ishtar, he used his increased strength to Shield Bash it away from him, unfortunately not stunning it. The other Hound was mere seconds behind, Ishtar mistimed the leap and missed it catching it with his shield being knocked back by its high strength and taking 50 damage as its claws found the opening between plates of his armour.

Ishtar used a Quick Thrust to ward off or skewer the Hound, seeing the one he had bashed away coming in from his side. This time he timed the leap right and warded off that dog again as he used his main magic ability and used Blades of Water inflicting a good amount of damage on the second Hound. His Rage was increasing which worried him that it might activate his Curse.

Ishtar was set waiting to be attacked by one of the two Hounds that were currently circling him. One tried to come in low but received a Cleave that was slightly late, taking off half its tail. When his attention was on that Hound, the other one came in low on the other side attacking his calf, trying to hamstring him. They may be Zombies and had lost all fear, but they had retained their ability to work in a pack and attack weak spots.

Continuing to defend against the Hounds whilst using Minor Heal to keep his health up, Ishtar struggled to inflict any major damage. Finally, one of the Hounds missed him as Ishtar stepped back to dodge the other one. It landed right in front of him. He used Quick Thrust through its head to inflict critical damage before pulling the sword out and slicing off its head without using another ability. Now that there was only one attacking him, Ishtar had a much easier time defending from it. The next time the Hound pounced on him Ishtar used Shield Bash and followed it as it hit the ground using Cleave to remove its head from its body.

Now that he had finished the Hounds that had attacked him Ishtar focused on Snow's fight with the bigger one. She had already killed the smaller Hound and was rolling across the ground with the Lead Hound, tearing each other apart. Ishtar used a Minor Heal on Snow. Due to her thicker fur and stronger skin preventing too much damage it refilled her Health completely. Ishtar moved to the blind spot of the Hound while it was completely focused on Snow and stabbed it through the leg getting its attention, Snow capitalised on this moment by clawing its face with a Light Claw before ripping out its throat.

Now that Ishtar and Snow had saved their own lives, Ishtar looked at the overall fight again. The Guards were down to only two against three Zombie Guards and a pair of Zombie Hounds, he hadn't seen before, so they had not gone down easily. Ishtar noticed his Rage stat was close to reaching its critical limit before he lost control. Hoping to finish the fight soon and prevent his curse from activating, he used Minor Heal on the remaining Guards as he and Snow moved to help them.

Focusing on the Hounds first, Ishtar managed to use Cleave to decapitate one while Snow brought the other down to the ground with her superior weight and ripped out its throat with Light Claw as she latched onto the back of its head breaking its neck.

While Ishtar and Snow had been taking care of the Hounds one of the Guards had been killed but not before taking out one of the Zombie Guards, this left the fight three against two in their favour. This time Ishtar and Snow focused on the same target, Snow attacking the legs with her Light Claw doing critical damage due to affinity, while Ishtar used Shield Bash to move it away from the Guard. This caused the Zombie Guard to fall over, Snow took the opportunity to pounce onto its arm and stop it from attacking as Ishtar dropped his Shield and used a 2H grip on his sword to Cleave. He didn't manage to completely remove the head of the Zombie Guard so while his sword was still in its neck, he activated Lightning Shock completely destroying its neck and a good portion of its jaw.

By the time they finished with that one, the last Zombie Guard had critically wounded the Guard and was just stabbing its sword through his eye. Everything around Ishtar seemed to pause for just a moment as he dropped to his knees.

"This is all my fault...I'm sorry, I'm so sorry. All of you." he barely whispered.

It was almost like his rage stat was waiting for this confession to break his mind a little before it reached the mark that the 'Curse of the Revenger' began.

Ishtar had no control over his body anymore. He felt himself stand up and look at Phillip who was still fighting with Captain Kieras.

"*Snow run!*" was all he could manage before the red that had been streaking across his eyes covered them completely. He was now just along for the ride as his rage and the Orb decided what happened. With the 500% increase to his mana regeneration beginning he healed himself and slowly started walking toward Phillip and Captain Kieras.

"YOU KILLED THEM ALL! I WILL DESTROY YOU!" Ishtar's voice went cold and venomous.

Both Captain Kieras and Phillip stopped their fight when they heard this voice, Ishtar saw that Captain Kieras's health was still dropping steadily while Phillip was looking thinner and paler.

"ARMAGEDDON".

A sea of red flames rocketed out of Ishtar and hit everything within a fifteen-metre radius, instantly burning all the Zombie corpses to ash and causing runes on Phillip's shield to activate. At first, the runes were a bright red that was repelling the increasing waves of fire that was being expelled out of Ishtar but were slowly dimming. Within ten seconds the flames had overwhelmed the enchantment on the shield and were hitting Phillip full on. Surprisingly, considering he was twenty levels lower, Ishtar was doing a good amount of damage and was starting to melt Phillip's armour from the intensity of the heat.

Suddenly Ishtar dropped to his knees almost completely out of mana even with the added regeneration of the Curse. This was when Snow returned from wherever she had fled. She seemed to appear next to Ishtar from nowhere as he regained the ability to control his body. He used Snow to stand back up and slowly started moving towards where

Phillip was still burning on the ground with the remains of his Armour melted into his body.

"My Lord will find you Ishtar! He told me what he was looking for and you clearly found it. Once he feels my death he will never stop hunting you, he wants those Orbs!" Phillip hissed.

"Fuck you and fuck him! So much death for his need for power...I'm doing the world a service with this." Ishtar replied with grief and anger tightening his voice.

Ishtar used Cleave to remove Phillip's head from his shoulders. Phillip's body quickly decomposed as soon as he died. Ishtar could only assume Phillip's disintegration was from the evil magic affecting his body.

Ishtar saw Captain Kieras with almost no health left either nearby. It was as if even when he saw Ishtar covered in the fire, he refused to move too far away in case Phillip escaped.

"Why Captain, why didn't you move away? I don't have enough mana after that to heal you, you have done so much for me, and this is how I repay you?" Ishtar rambled.

"Stop, this isn't your fault. Phillip was always going to try and kill me one day, and this time he coated his sword with a deadly poison, so I was never going to walk away today." Captain Kieras admitted.

He then reached into his belt pouch and removed a sealed letter, he forced this letter into Ishtar's hand before continuing.

"You must take this to the King. It has all the proof I have against Lord Doorakian, and this ambush by his most loyal follower will be further proof. I need you to do this for me, my friend..." Captain Kieras declared and just as he said 'Friend' he slipped away into death.

Ishtar placed the letter in his inventory without paying attention, he couldn't see due to the tears running down his face. He felt a large body rub against him as he cried for what felt like hours.

Finally, Ishtar stood up and felt a sense of resolve tighten in his chest. He couldn't let these men that died for him be left on this battlefield. Ishtar spent the next hour collecting wood to build a funeral pyre before moving the seven bodies of the brave men onto the top. He grabbed a stick out of the still burning fire and lit the pyre, Ishtar stood there stock still with Snow at his side watching the flames until dawn started to break over the horizon.

Just as the dawn light hit the pyre, a bright light engulfed the pyre, and it disappeared into motes of light. A single tear fell down Ishtar's cheek as he saw that whichever God had taken the bodies had left a bag on the ground.

Before checking what was in the bag Ishtar decided to check his notifications.

You are once again the last survivor of a battle
You have gained the title: The Survivor
Any being that has ever served in a military will show you respect as they see the ghosts of all those that died at your side in your eyes, just as you can see it in theirs.
Fame increased by 1000

In conjunction with Captain Kieras and a Squad of Gate Guards you have successfully killed:
Zombie Hound x15
Zombie Guard x6
Lord Guard Captain Phillip (Unique) x1
You and your familiar have gained 91,500 Exp each as the only surviving participants of the fight

Congratulations!
You have gained a level x3
You are now Level 18
+12 Str, +12 Int, +6 Vit and 12 Free stat points.

Congratulations!
Your Familiar has gained a level x5
She is now Level 14
+10 Str, +10 Agi, +10 Vit, +20 Int, +10 End and 10 Free stat points.

You have been given a non-refusable quest!
*Deliver Captain Kieras's letter to the King and Report the
ambush.*
Reward:
????
Failure:
????

Ishtar picked up the bag and started walking
towards Cindera and the future.

Epilogue

The Lamia Water Orb Wielder sat on her new throne made from the bones of the beasts that keep spawning on the Island of human cannibals she had taken over.

She looked around her throne room: to her Elite Level fifty guards, her pool of water nearby for her to manipulate, and finally back to the prisoner kneeling before her. It wasn't like she could do much more to torture him; he was already unable to run away missing his legs as, apparently, the men on the boat had been hungry.

"Tell me about the defences to Cindera's harbour, as you can see we are a bit short on metals." her deep melodious voice rang out.

The Catfolk man flinched at her voice but kept to his duty, his only reply was spitting on the ground at her feet. This earned him a smack on the head from the guard behind him. The guard was raising her arm to hit him again before the Lamia raised her hand to stop her.

"Fine let's do it your way" she answered.

Manipulating the water in her pool, the Lamia pulled out an orb of water and floated it towards the prisoner's head. She kept it close to his head and waited for the fear to show on his face before she moved the orb over his head. Watching him struggle not to breathe a smile appeared on the Lamia's face. Once it looked like he was about to drown she removed the orb from his head and asked her question again.

It took five repetitions of this before he started talking, and as soon as he finished talking, he started screaming as he was dragged away by the hungry looking cannibals.

*

The Wood Elf Earth Orb Wielder was running through the streets of a big city. He knew that assassins were hunting him, he dropped into closest the alleyway and stuck his back against the wall just a metre in.

He activated his concealment. It worked just as well in the big city as it did when he was in the forests. Just because he was a Ranger, people seemed to assume he was only dangerous at a distance, they forgot that ranger's come with dual wield. Getting ready for the Assassin who should soon get there, the Elf touched his hands to the ground and pulled coming up with a pair of daggers made from obsidian,

"The beauty of the Lost Continent having dormant volcanoes is all the fun items in the ground," he thought to himself, not for the first time.

He could feel a presence in the stone building above him, but it hadn't moved since it had reached the roof. He then felt a half dozen presences closing off each end of the alleyway. He knew the person above him was the assassin, but the others were probably just thugs being used as a distraction. Only one was left at each end while the other four were sent down to attack him.

Since he could feel they were coming through the earth, the Elf waited until the thugs were just about close enough before leaping from the shadow of concealment and stabbing the closest pair through the eyes, instantly killing them with his level and strength advantage. Unable to reuse those he touched the ground to pull another pair of daggers out of the dirt, this time he didn't want to kill them both, he wanted information. He threw both daggers at the other pair of thugs, hitting one in the leg while missing the other. The Elf advanced slowly at the one he missed with a new set of daggers, these thugs were well below his level.

One of the thugs tried to attack him with his sword, the elf ducked under it and stabbed both daggers into the thug's unprotected face. It was then he felt the presence on the roof disappear and a presence behind him emerge, with no daggers left he touched the stone wall beside him as he turned to pull a short sword out of the wall, just in time to parry the blow dart that had been shot at him.

The assassin seeing his attack had failed deemed his mission a failure. The target was too strong for him and that had been the last of his poison, he had been hunting the target all night and kept failing to poison him. The assassin disappeared in a puff of black smoke as the Elf felt his presence recede in the distance. The Elf went back to the remaining thug on the ground,

"Who hired you to hunt me?" the Elf asked.

"It's not just you, they just wanted the Orb…everyone seems to want those damn Orbs," the thug replied.

The Elf swore, he knew that he should never have been studying the Orb in public, but once he could summon it at will he was curious.

"Who in particular hired you lot?" the Elf asked again.

"Some Lord has a standing bounty on any information on the Orbs. We figured he would pay us even more if we could get the Orb ourselves." the Thug explained.

The Elf pulled his original blade rather than one of his created ones and slit the thug's throat before climbing up the building next to him making hand holds with his earth manipulation.

*

Justice was watching his newly "convinced" recruits combat a dungeon boss. These Dungeons on the Lost Continent had been useful to him. With their cores at the centre, it became a continuous dungeon, only a few hours till the whole place respawned its monsters after defeat. These ones didn't want to help him but since finding the Air Orb it had become much easier to compel people to help him, a little bit of blackmail or using his new abilities and the Charm stat that came with it also helped with NPC's.

He now had officially started a Guild in the North Neutral City and all members were subject to his whims. He even put it in the charter that he personally got 15% of their loot. Justice had found he liked having power over others, he was starting to respect his father for effortlessly manipulating people for years to gain and retain power. He had been following his father's instructions for a while now, but he wanted to own this world all on his own.

As the Dungeon boss got too low in health a flood of arrows came out the walls aimed at the warriors attacking, Justice saw that the ones with the shields were out of place and unable to protect their casters.

"Useless, all of you" he uttered as he waved his hand and a wall of air intercepted the arrows.

He suddenly heard a voice behind him.

"Justice we have a problem, the City Lord is trying to make decisions on his own." a being clad entirely in black announced.

"Fine, I will have to go have another talk with him," Justice answered.

"Hmm so charm has a limit, their willpower can combat it over time if I don't reinforce it," he thought as he started for the exit.

*

Lord Doorakian felt his disciple Phillip burn, filled with rage at the audacity of that traveller not only to lie to him, but to destroy his pets and a useful slave.

He clicked his fingers and a shadow rose off the floor, an almost human shape was formed.

"Find the traveller for me" he ordered.

The shadow man didn't make any motion of acknowledgement, just disappeared into the floor.

"I will have those Orbs" Lord Doorakian announced.

Many floors below ground skeletons, zombies and other abominations awaited their creator's command.

FIN

Final Status

Status
Name: *Ishtar*
Alignment: *Good*
Level: 18   **Exp:** *26,400/41,000*
Class: *Elemental Knight*
Race: *Elemental Draconian*
Money: *74G 45S 75C* **Gender:** *Male*
Title: *Seeker of the Hidden III*
Chosen of Thia
The Survivor
Fame: *1560*   **Infamy:** *0*

-

Health: *710/710*   **Health Regen:** *35.3/Sec*
Mana: *1070/1070*   **Mana Regen:** *31.0/Sec*
Stamina: *550/550*   **Stamina Regen:** *66.0/Sec*

-

Strength: *77 (118)*   **Dexterity:** *25 (31)*
Agility: *27 (43)*   **Endurance:** *38 (55)*
Vitality: *51 (66)*   **Intelligence:** *78 (107)*
Wisdom: *23 (29)*   **Luck:** *12 (16)*
Free Stat Points: *20*

-

Affinity:
Water: 100%
Air: 100%
Earth: 100%
Light: 100%
Lightning: 100%
Ice: 100%

Arcane: 100%
Fire: 100%

-

Orbs

Fire

-

Abilities:
Active
Blades of Water Basic Level 3
Cleave Basic Level 3
Shield Bash Beginner Level 7
Guard Beginner Level 8
Quick Thrust Beginner Level 9
Wind Strike Beginner Level 8
Metal Coat Basic Level 1
Minor Heal Beginner Level 8
Mana Bolt Beginner Level 4
Lightning Shock Beginner Level 3
Ice Dagger Beginner Level 4
Fire Eyes Beginner Level 6
Armageddon Beginner Level 3
Passive
1H Weapon Proficiency Basic Level 3
Heavy Armour Proficiency Basic Level 4
Shield Proficiency Basic Level 2
Mana Manipulation Beginner Level 9

-

Skills:

Mining Beginner Level 5
Appraisal Basic Level 1
Meditation Basic Level 1
Mana Sense Beginner Level 5

Minor Poison Resistance Beginner Level 1
Repair Beginner Level 6

Status
Name: *Snow*
Race: *Light Direwolf (Variant)*
Level: *14*
Experience: *4150/30000*
Health: *400/400* **Health Regen:** *2 5.4/ Sec*
Mana: *530/530* **Mana Regen:** *39.0/ Sec*
Stamina: *370/370* **Stamina Regen:** *40.0/ Sec*
-

Strength: *45* **Dexterity:** *32*
Agility: *52* **Endurance :** *37*
Vitality: *40* **Intelligence:** *53*
Wisdom: *36* **Luck:** *19*
Free Stat Points: *10*

Current Quests

Quest Received! - Head-hunter
You have killed 2 enemies Execution style. Once you have killed 50, go to the temple of Vames to receive your prize.
Reward:
A title from the God of Death and Darkness
Progress:
12/50

Legendary Quest Received!
The exiled Goddess Thiadria has requested you find or take from your competitors the six Sacred Elemental Orbs, that each contain a portion of her power, and take them to her first temple to release the contained portion of the world and herself back into the universe.
Note: if completed you will change the face of the world.
Reward:
Unknown
Progress:
1/6

Quest Accepted!
Goblin Extermination
D Rank Quest
Goblins have been spotted in the forest between River City and Cindera.
They pose a threat to the merchants that use this route.
Kill any you find to maintain public safety.
Reward:
50S

Quest Accepted!
Direwolf Culling
D Rank Quest
Direwolves have been spotted in the forest between River City and Cindera.
They pose a threat to the merchants that use this route.
Kill any you find to maintain public safety.
Reward:
50S

You have been given a non-refusable quest!
Deliver Captain Kieras's letter to the King and Report the ambush.
Reward:
????
Failure:
????

<u>Current Gear</u>

Pendant of Clotier
Type: *Jewellery* **Durability:** *45/50*
Quality: *Rare*
Clotier was a Mage, with a deathly fear of Rodents. His Adventuring group forced him to enter these tunnels, looking for the Rodent King.
+8 to Intelligence
+2 per second to Mana Recover

Minor Ring of Health
Type: *Jewellery* **Durability:** *30/30*
Quality: *Uncommon*
A weak magic ring
+50 Health

Minor Ring of Armour Negation
Type: *Jewellery* **Durability:** *30/30*
Quality: *Uncommon*
A weak magic ring
-10% to Heavy Armour mana interference

Iron Elemental Broadsword
Type: *Broadsword* **Durability:** *100/100*
Quality: *Uncommon* **Damage:** *15-25*
+20 to all Affinities
+10 Str
+5 Int

A well-made iron blade made specifically for an Elemental Knight

Foreman's Steel Pickaxe
Type: *Pickaxe* **Durability:** *150/150*
Quality: *Rare* **Damage:** *15-25*
+10 to Mining
+15 Str
Increase Mining Speed by 45%
Unable to be used in combat
A very rare Pickaxe that was specifically made for Foreman Aniga of the Miditarac Iron Mine

Nymph Staff
Type: *Staff* **Durability:** *80/80*
Quality: *Rare* **Damage:** *10-15*
A Wizard's staff made from the remains of a Nymph's Tree home.
+15 to Intelligence
+ 25% Damage to Earth and Nature Spells

Ishtar's Wolf Helmet
Type: *Helmet* **Durability:** *500/500*
Quality: *Epic* **Defence:** *75*
The Helmet in the unique set of Armour created by the Expert blacksmith for the Adventurer Ishtar. Created using metal grown by a monster and the legendary metal Electrum.
Full Set Bonus: +10 Agility
Enchantment:
Faceshield

Ishtar's Wolf Chestplate
Type: *Chestplate* **Durability:** *500/500*
Quality: *Epic* **Defence:** *200*
The Chestplate in the unique set of Armour created by the Expert blacksmith for the Adventurer Ishtar. Created using metal grown by a monster and the legendary metal Electrum.
Full Set Bonus: +10 Intelligence
Enchantments:
Increased Durability
Increased Defence

Ishtar's Wolf Gauntlets
Type: *Gauntlets* **Durability:** *500/500*
Quality: *Epic* **Defence:** *75*
The Gauntlets in the unique set of Armour created by the Expert blacksmith for the Adventurer Ishtar. Created using metal grown by a monster and the legendary metal Electrum
Attack Damage: 25-50
Full Set Bonus: +10 Strength
Enchantments:
Decreased Mana Cost
Increased Magic Damage

Ishtar's Wolf Greaves
Type: *Greaves* **Durability:** *500/500*
Quality: *Epic* **Defence:** *150*
The Greaves in the unique set of Armour created by the Expert blacksmith for the Adventurer Ishtar. Created using metal grown by a monster and the legendary metal Electrum.
Full Set Bonus: +10 Vitality
Enchantment:
Decreased Weight

Ishtar's Wolf Boots
Type: *Boots* **Durability:** *500/500*
Quality: *Epic* **Defence:** *75*

The pair of Boots in the unique set of Armour created by the Expert blacksmith for the Adventurer Ishtar. Created using metal grown by a monster and the legendary metal Electrum.
Full Set Bonus: + 10 Endurance

Enchantment:
Increased Movement Speed

Thank you.

I hope you have enjoyed *A Piece of Legend*. Book two will hopefully not take too long.

If you have questions or comments, you can contact me through my,

Patreon: https://www.patreon.com/anuzan

Facebook Page https://www.facebook.com/Craig-Dunn-Author-975355845961743